THE
GIRLS' GUIDE
TO HUNTING
AND FISHING

MELISSA BANK

PENGUIN BOOKS

PENGUIN BOOKS

Published by the Penguin Group
Penguin Books Ltd, 27 Wrights Lane, London W8 5TZ, England
Penguin Putnam Inc., 375 Hudson Street, New York, New York 10014, USA
Penguin Books Australia Ltd, Ringwood, Victoria, Australia
Penguin Books Canada Ltd, 10 Alcorn Avenue, Toronto, Ontario, Canada M4V 3B2
Penguin Books (NZ) Ltd, Private Bag 102902, NSMC, Auckland, New Zealand

Penguin Books Ltd, Registered Offices: Harmondsworth, Middlesex, England

First published by Viking 1999
Published in Penguin Books 2000

1

Some of the stories in this book first appeared in the following publications:
"Advanced Beginners" (as "Lucky You") in *The North American Review*; "The Floating
House" in *Another Chicago Magazine*; "My Old Man" (as "Dennis the Menace and Mr.
Wilson" in *Chicago Tribune*; "The Best Possible Light" in *Other Voices*; and "The Girls'
Guide to Hunting and Fishing" in *Zoetrope: All-Story*.

Grateful acknowledgment is made for permission to reprint "One Art" from *The
Complete Poems 1927–1979* by Elizabeth Bishop. Copyright © 1979, 1983 by Alice
Helen Methfessel. Reprinted by permission of Farrar, Straus & Giroux, Inc.; and "The
Commuter's Lament or A Close Shave" by Norman B. Colp. Copyright © Norman B.
Colp, 1991. Reprinted by permission of the author.

Printed in England by Clays Ltd, St Ives plc

TO MY REAL-LIFE GIRL GUIDES

Adrienne Brodeur, Carole DeSanti,
Carol Fiorino, Molly Friedrich,
Judy Katz, and Anna Wingfield

The art of losing isn't hard to master;
so many things seem filled with the intent
to be lost that their loss is no disaster.

Lose something every day. Accept the fluster
of lost door keys, the hour badly spent.
The art of losing isn't hard to master.

Then practice losing farther, losing faster:
places, and names, and where it was you meant
to travel. None of these will bring disaster.

I lost my mother's watch. And look! my last, or
next-to-last, of three loved houses went.
The art of losing isn't hard to master.

I lost two cities, lovely ones. And, vaster,
some realms I owned, two rivers, a continent.
I miss them, but it wasn't a disaster.

—Even losing you (the joking voice, a gesture
I love) I shan't have lied. It's evident
the art of losing's not too hard to master
though it may look like (*Write* it!) like disaster.

"One Art," from *The Complete Poems 1927–1979,*
by Elizabeth Bishop

ACKNOWLEDGMENTS

Thanks to Alexandra Babanskyj, Barbara Grossman, Susan Petersen, and Paul Slovak at Viking; to Francis Coppola, Karla Eoff, Alicia Patterson, Samantha Schnee, and Joanna Yas at *Zoetrope: All Story*; to Kathy Minton and Isaiah Sheffer at Selected Shorts; to Lucy Childs and Paul Cirone at the Aaron Priest Literary Agency; to my trusty readers—Michael Atmore, Joan Bank, Donna Barba, Margery Bates, Scott Bryson, Arthur Chernoff, Paul Cody, Jane Dickinson, Hunter Hill, Mitch Karsh, Ken Katz, Peter Landesman, Alex Moon, Jane Moriarty, Sylvie Rabineau, Michael Ruby, Oren Rudavsky, Julie Schumacher, Sandy Stillman, Joe Sweet, John Szalay, Jack Wetling, Judy Wohl—and especially Garth Wingfield, who helped me with every version of every story; and, finally, thanks to my brother, Andrew Bank, for listening to all the boring details, making me laugh every day, and always coming to the rescue.

CONTENTS

ADVANCED

BEGINNERS

———————————

While home is the place where you can relax and be yourself, this doesn't mean that you can take advantage of the love and affection other members of your family have for you.

—From *20th Century Typewriting* by D. D. Lessenberry, T. James Crawford, and Lawrence W. Erickson

My brother's first serious girlfriend was eight years older—twenty-eight to his twenty. Her name was Julia Cathcart, and Henry introduced her to us in early June. They drove from Manhattan down to our cottage in Loveladies, on the New Jersey shore. When his little convertible, his pet, pulled into the driveway, she was behind the wheel. My mother and I were watching from the kitchen window. I said, "He lets her drive his car."

My brother and his girlfriend were dressed alike, baggy white shirts tucked into jeans, except she had a black cashmere sweater over her shoulders.

She had dark eyes, high cheekbones, and beautiful skin, pale, with high coloring in her cheeks like a child with a fever. Her hair was back in a loose ponytail, tied with a piece of lace, and she wore tiny pearl earrings.

I thought maybe she'd look older than Henry, but it was Henry who looked older than Henry. Standing there, he looked like a man. He'd grown a beard, for starters, and had on new wire-rim sunglasses that made him appear more like a bon vivant than a philosophy major between colleges. His hair was longer, and, not yet lightened by the sun, it was the reddish-brown color of an Irish setter.

He gave me a kiss on the cheek, as though he always had.

Then he roughed around with our Airedale, Atlas, while his girlfriend and mother shook hands. They were clasping fingertips, ladylike, smiling as though they were already fond of each other and just waiting for details to fill in why.

Julia turned to me and said, "You must be Janie."

"Most people call me Jane now," I said, making myself sound even younger.

"Jane," she said, possibly in the manner of an adult trying to take a child seriously.

Henry unpacked the car and loaded himself up with everything they'd brought, little bags and big ones, a string tote, and a knapsack.

As he started up the driveway, his girlfriend said, "Do you have the wine, Hank?"

Whoever Hank was, he had it.

Except for bedrooms and the screened-in porch, our house was just one big all-purpose room, and Henry was giving her a jokey tour of it: "This is the living room," he said, gesturing to the sofa; he paused, gestured to it again and said, "This is the den."

Out on the porch, she stretched her legs in front of

her—Audrey Hepburn relaxing after dance class. She wore navy espadrilles. I noticed that Henry had on penny Loafers without socks, and he'd inserted a subway token in the slot where the penny belonged.

Julia sipped her iced tea and asked how Loveladies got its name. We didn't know, but Henry said, "It was derived from the Indian name of the founder."

Julia smiled, and asked my mother how long we'd been coming here.

"This is our first year," my mother said.

My father was out playing tennis, and without him present, I felt free to add a subversive, "We used to go to Nantucket."

"Nantucket is lovely," Julia said.

"It is lovely," my mother conceded, but went on to cite drab points in New Jersey's favor, based on its proximity to our house in Philadelphia.

In the last of our New Jersey versus Nantucket debates, I'd argued, forcefully I'd thought, that Camden was even closer. I'd almost added that the trash dump was practically in walking distance, but my father had interrupted.

I could tell he was angry, but he kept his voice even: we could go to the shore all year round, he said, and that would help us to be a closer family.

"Not so far," I said, meaning to add levity.

But my father looked at me with his eyes narrowed, like he wasn't sure I was his daughter after all.

My mother smiled at me and said that the house was

right on the water! I'd be able to walk right out the door and go swimming!

Only then did I understand that they'd already chosen a house; they'd put a bid on it.

"It's on the ocean?" I asked.

"Close," she said, trying to maintain her enthusiasm.

"The bay," I said to myself.

"It does have a spectacular view of the bay," she said, but, no, our house was on a lagoon, a canal. "Like Venice," she'd said, as though this would mean something to me.

Now Julia asked if we swam in there, and my mother said, "Absolutely."

I didn't want to acid rain on my mother's parade, but the lagoon had oil floating on the surface and the bottom was sewagey soft.

I was surprised how long Henry sat with us on the porch, as my mother turned the topic to summer, touching upon such controversial issues as corn on the cob (Silver Queen was best), mosquitoes (pesky), and tennis (good exercise).

Finally, Henry did get up. He went outside as though on a mission. He might be going to check my crab traps or to see if we'd brought the bikes; he could do whatever he wanted. My father was the same way: a houseful of guests, and my mother's duty was to provide food, drink, fun, and conversation, while my father's was to nap or read.

While Mother hostessed and Girlfriend guested,

Younger Sister stood up. When there was a pause in their nicing, I made my mouth move smileward: *I'd love to stay and talk, but I have to go shoot some heroin now.*

———•———

For dinner, we had crabs I'd caught off the dock. My mother covered the table with newspaper, and we all got print on our arms. As a surprise, she served preseason Silver Queen, little nuggets of mush. My brother ate his like a normal person, instead of typewriter-style; usually, he'd tap the cob at the end of a row and ding.

In response to my mother's questions, Julia told us about her brother in San Francisco and sister in Paris, both of whom would be "attending" her mother's annual "gala" in Southampton. Julia chose her words carefully and used ones I'd never heard spoken—she sounded to me like she was trying out for a job as a dictionary.

My mother eyed me: *Do not smirk.*

However slowly Julia spoke, she opened her crabs twice as fast as anyone else, and I asked how she did it. She showed me the key on the belly side and how to pull it so the shell lifted right off. Henry leaned over to watch, too.

My father asked about the publishing house where she and Henry worked. Julia described their boss as an exquisite editor and true gentleman. My brother had a laugh-smile on when he said, "Every morning when we're opening the mail, Mr. McBride comes into subrights and says, 'Did we get any dough, babies?' "

I'd met this exquisite editor and true gentleman

myself when I'd visited Henry; and I repeated now that Mr. McBride had told me my brother "Aaron" was irreplaceable.

My father said, "Hank Aaron," almost to himself.

"Mr. McBride must be forgiven," Julia said, "as a baseball aficionado and octogenarian."

I thought, *Exquisite octogenarians and aficionados will be attending the gala.*

Then I asked my question: "Do they know about you two at work?"

My father shot me a look; and I looked back at him, *Why is everything I want to know wrong?*

Henry changed the topic: he'd been promoted from intern to assistant. I could tell he expected my parents to be pleased, and I saw right away that my father, at least, wasn't. It was harder to tell with my mother; she wore the mask in the family.

The issue, I realized, was college. Henry still hadn't decided if he was starting Columbia in the fall.

He'd already transferred four times, or five counting twice to Brown. The reasons he gave for transferring each time were always sound and logical, like "better course selection." I wondered about the reasons he didn't say.

———•———

Before bed, my mother told Julia she'd be staying with me—my cue. I led her down the hall to my bedroom, which was completely taken up by a built-in bunk-bed complex; it slept four but, I realized, lived only one comfortably.

"A bunk," she said, as though charmed. "Like camp."

A cell, I thought. *Like prison.*

I asked which bunk she wanted; she chose the near bottom, which meant the far top for me. I got fresh towels for her and left her alone to undress; then I knocked on my door, and she said, "Come in."

She was already under the covers, so I turned out the light. I climbed up to my bunk and swept the sand off my sheets. We said good night. After a few minutes, though, a door slammed, and I had to explain that the doorjambs in this house didn't stick; the doors would be opening and slamming all night. Then "good night"— "good night" again.

I closed my eyes and tried to pretend I was in Nantucket.

The house we'd rented every year there had a widow's walk—a square porch on the roof, where the wives of sea captains were supposed to have watched for their husbands' ships. At night, we'd hear creaks and moans. Once, I thought I heard footsteps pacing the widow's walk. You could feel the ghosts in that house, scaring you in the best way.

If there were any ghosts in this one, they weren't moaning about husbands lost at sea but slamming doors over modern, trivial matters, such as not being allowed to go waterskiing.

I couldn't sleep with Julia down there, and I could tell she couldn't sleep either. We lay awake in the dark, listening to each other. The silence between us seemed both intimate and hostile, like a staring contest. But Julia was just waiting for me to fall asleep so she could go down the hall to my brother's room. I heard her bare feet on the wood floor and Henry's door whisper open and close.

——•——

My father and Henry went to look at sailboats to buy, though I suspected talk about Columbia.

My mother, Julia, and I took a walk on the beach. I walked behind them, in and out of the water, looking for sea glass. My mother was describing the exhibit we'd happened on the last time we were in New York—dishes, silverware, and crystal used by royalty—and Julia had seen the exhibit herself, on purpose.

The museum was like the house of a rich old woman who didn't want you to visit; everyone had whispered and stepped lightly, as though trying to pretend they weren't really there. The guest book requested comments, and my mother, who never missed a chance to compliment anyone, had written how finely curated the exhibit was. I'd written, "Bored nearly to death."

I experienced this anew listening to them talk tableware. They loved the same plates for the same reasons with the same enthusiasm, and I thought, *Henry is going out with Mom.*

——•——

When I told Henry, he said, "My sister the Freudian."

Julia was doing my jobs in the kitchen, setting the table and helping her soul twin prepare an early supper.

I was sitting on Henry's bed, while he packed to go

back to New York. He always did something else while we talked—changed the station on the radio, flipped through a magazine, tuned his guitar. He didn't have to look at me; he knew I'd still be there, with my next question.

"You should read Freud," he said, and went to his bookshelf to see if he had any Freud handy. He didn't, but went on saying what a great writer Freud was, as though this was what I wanted to talk about in our only moments alone all weekend.

I remembered to thank him for the last book he'd sent to me from work, by a Norwegian philosopher, and he said, "Did you try it?"

"Yeah," I said, "I spent about a month reading it one afternoon."

He turned to me and said, "Do you know that your IQ goes up and down about fifty points in every conversation?"

I didn't know if this was a compliment or an insult, but I didn't like how he was looking at me—as though from the great distance of his new life. I said, "No one likes being talked about to their face." Then I felt bad. "Anyway," I said, "$E = MC^2$."

Henry smiled and opened a drawer. He told me that he'd gone to hear the Norwegian lecture. "Imagine trying to understand that philosophy through the thickest accent you've ever heard," he said. "Now add a harelip."

But everyone was pretending to understand the lecture, he said, and he imitated serious note scribbling.

Then he interrupted himself—he'd spotted Freud on the bottom shelf.

He flipped through the book for the passage he wanted me to hear and found it. "Okay, Freud says: 'In sending the young out into life with such a false psychological orientation' about sex, it's 'as though one were to equip people starting out on a Polar expedition with summer clothes and maps of the Italian lakes.' " He shook his head. "And that's a footnote," he said. "A footnote."

I said, "You look like Commodore Peary with your beard."

He touched his face, absently, the way bearded men do. Then he handed the book—*Civilization and Its Discontents*—to me.

"So," I said, "does Julia talk about exquisite plates when you're alone?"

He told me to go easy on Julia; she was nervous about meeting Mom and Dad. "Try to think of it from her side."

I decided I would later.

He picked a purple shirt out of his closet. "Want this?" He tossed it to me. "I bought it at a thrift shop in Berkeley," he said, referring to his last internship, a behavior-modification lab where he'd trained herd dogs not to herd.

I said, "I think I saw you more when you lived there."

He told me that he and Julia would come to the shore again in a few weeks.

"I might not recognize you by then," I said. "You'll probably show up in a suit and tie."

"What are you talking about?"

"You seem older," I said.

"I am older."

"Three months shouldn't make this much of a difference," I said. "Your whole personality has changed."

Finally, he stopped and looked at me.

"You're Hank now," I said. "You bring Mom and Dad a bottle of wine."

Then he sat down on the bed with me. "I might be growing up," he said. "I'm probably not, but let's say I am. Is that a reason to be mad at me?"

I looked at the purple shirt in my lap. It had a big ink stain on the pocket.

Then Julia called us to dinner.

"Come on," he said.

Dinner: talk of great books everyone had read or planned to, except me. Julia had just read one by a famous author I'd never heard of and proclaimed it "extraordinary." I thought, *You read too much.*

At good-bye, I could tell how much both my parents liked her, and not just for Henry's sake; Julia was the kind, helpful, articulate daughter they deserved.

———•———

On the ride home, I thought about Julia. I calculated what an eight-year age difference would mean to me—a six-year-old boy—and thought of the one next door. I said, "It's like me going out with Willy Schwam."

My mother pretended not to hear.

I could hear the smile in my father's voice when he said that the important thing was that Willy and I were happy.

"I was dubious at first," I said. "I thought I might be just another baby-sitter to him. But then, one night—"

My mother interrupted. "I think I'm going to be ill."

I never talked to either of my parents seriously about love, let alone sex. The closest we'd come was talking about drugs, which I wasn't interested in.

———•———

On the last day of school, I realized I had no plans for the summer. Instead of looking forward to Nantucket in August, I'd be at home in the suburbs and at the shore in New Jersey, just dreading school in September.

I said good-bye to friends who were going off on wilderness adventures and teen tours, to camps with Indian names and Israel. We traded addresses and each time I wrote mine I felt the impending boredom of the summer days to come. When one friend asked what I'd be doing at home, I found myself saying, "I might get a job."

I told my parents at dinner.

My mother said, "I thought you were going to take art classes and work on your tennis."

"I could get a part-time job," I said.

"Maybe you could work in Dad's office again," she said, looking over at him.

I liked seeing Dad in action, the Chief of Neurology in his white coat, as he shook patients' hands and ushered them into his office. But I said, "I need new experiences, Mom."

"What about an internship," she suggested, "in something you're interested in?"

I reminded her that I didn't have any interests.

"You like to draw," she said.

I told them I was thinking of being a waitress.

My dad said, "Practice by clearing the table."

—— • ——

I went through the help wanted section of the newspaper, but every job seemed to require experience. I called anyway to make my case, using the words I read in the paper: "I'm a detail-oriented self starter." No luck, though. I gave in to a summer of art classes and tennis, swimming at my friend Linda's, and going on errands with my mother.

The nights were quiet. Dinner, and then I went up to my bedroom and wrote letters to my friends or sketched. I drew people standing in groups, as though posed for a photograph that would go in an album.

My father read his magazines, the green-covered *Neurology* and *Stroke,* up in his study. My mother read the newspaper in the breakfast room. She would call up to him, asking if he wanted a piece of fruit, and I'd go downstairs and back up to deliver the peach or plum or nectarine. Before bed, I walked Atlas, while I smoked a forbidden cigarette.

Most nights, I passed Oliver Biddle, who was middle-aged, yet lived with his parents—my own personal cautionary tale walking a miniature schnauzer. He was suburban-soft in stretchy clothes a grandfather would wear for golf, and he puffed a cigar. I'd heard rumors that he was retarded or a genius, but I didn't believe either. Oliver Biddle was who you became if you couldn't find anyone to love except your parents.

I'd say, "Hello, Oliver," and then, to his schnauzer, "Evening, Pepper."

Oliver said hello back, but always after a delay, as though each time deciding whether to answer. By the time he did, I'd be at least a few steps away and I'd say, "Good night," as though we'd passed the evening together.

———•———

Julia and Henry got out early on Fridays and were already at the shore when we arrived. She'd made dinner, and seemed more relaxed. Henry seemed hardly to have aged at all.

After dessert, they invited me to go with them to the arts center for a Russian film with English subtitles.

I said, "I don't like to read during movies," and once Julia laughed it became a joke and made me feel that I was irrepressibly witty. So I went with them.

It was the bleakest movie I'd ever seen; everyone died of heartbreak or starvation or both. At home, Julia threw herself on the sofa in Slavic despair and said, "Please to get me some wodka."

They didn't kiss or hold hands in front of me, though once, at lunch, Henry sort of rubbed my foot under the table, thinking it was Julia's. I leaned over to him and whispered, "You're really turning me on." I was a teenager, after all, an expert in the art of mortification.

———•———

At the beach, we left our sandals and sneakers on the path with the other shoes, and spread our towels on the sand, facing the ocean. Henry stood a minute looking out, then bounded into the water.

The ocean was rough, and as the waves rose you could see clear jellyfish and green popping seaweed. Up where we were, clumps of seaweed had dried almost black in the sun. The wind blew so strong that the seaweed whipped loose and rolled down the beach like tumbleweeds.

I looked around us at the people on the beach. A group of women my mother's age wore bikinis and gold bracelets and were already deeply tanned. The really thin ones looked mean. A small community had set up chairs near our towels. A man was pouring something clear out of a thermos into outstretched plastic glasses, while a woman passed a Baggie of lime wedges.

Julia wore a blousy white beach dress and a big straw hat, and slathered herself in sunscreen though she stayed in the shade under an umbrella. She was reading, as usual.

"You seem to really like your job," I said.

She nodded. Then she asked me if I had any idea what I wanted to do when I grew up.

"I'd like to be a great singer," I said.

"Maybe you will," she said.

"I won't."

"How do you know?"

"Tone-deaf," I said.

I sat up on my elbows, watching Henry in the ocean. The water was just getting warm, and he was the only one in for a while. He waited for his wave in a standstill crawl position, his body facing us, but his head turned back to where the waves formed. Then he swam hard, caught the wave, and rode it all the way in to shore. I loved how he looked the last second of his ride—his hair sluiced back, his part zigzagged, his face pure joy. Sometimes he would actually laugh out loud. When he stood up, he'd look toward us, but he couldn't see without his glasses.

I joined him in the ocean. It was cold, but I kept up with him and went under when he did. I stood beside him, and he pulled my arms out in front of me. He'd been trying to teach me to bodysurf for years. "Now wait for your wave." He looked behind him. "Swim hard," he said suddenly. "Now!"

But I missed that wave, and the next one. Then Julia came in. The two of them swam beyond where the waves broke, and I got out.

On my towel, I watched them bob with the swell of the wave just forming. Then he dove under. He pointed his hand out of the water, like a shark fin, and went after her. I saw her arms flailing as she was pulled under.

The next time I looked up, she was coming toward me. Before she put on her beach dress, I got a good look at her figure. She had on a black one-piece and was even thinner than I suspected, with smaller breasts than I had.

That year, all of a sudden it seemed, there my breasts were, and my mother and I kept having to go to Lord & Taylor for bigger bras. Boys gave me more attention now, and it made me nervous. My breasts seemed to say something about me that I didn't want said. My Achilles' heel, they put me in constant danger of humiliation.

My theory was that if you had breasts, boys wanted to have sex with you, which wasn't exactly a big compliment, since they wanted to have sex anyway. Whereas if you had a beautiful face, like Julia, boys fell in love with you, which seemed to happen almost against their will. Then the sex that you had would be about love.

I'd told my theory to my friend Linda, who wanted to be a social scientist and was always coming up with theories herself. I'd concluded that breasts were to sex what pillows were to sleep. "Guys might think they want a pillow, but they'll sleep just as well without one."

She'd said, "Guys will sleep anywhere if they're really tired."

————•————

That night, when Julia got into her bunk, I told her that she could go into Henry's now if she wanted; she didn't have to wait for me to fall asleep. I said, "I think I might be older than you think I am."

She stopped, and seemed to be choosing her words. I wanted her to know she didn't have to do this either, but I couldn't think how to say it without insulting her.

She admitted that she didn't really know anyone my age. "I keep trying to remember what I was like at fourteen," she said. "Other than books, I think all I cared about was my horse, Cinders."

I pictured her in one of those black velvet hats with the little bows on top. I said, "What happened to Cinders?"

"Boys?" She smiled at me. Then we said good night and she went to my brother's room.

In the middle of the night, on my way to the bathroom, I noticed that his door had blown open. Before I closed it, I saw them in his single bed, sleeping in a loose hug, his arms holding her bare back.

——•——

A few weekends later, the sky was white and the air moist; the forecast was rain, but my mother kept looking up at the sky and saying it was sure to clear up.

In the afternoon, Julia sat at the table, marking up a manuscript from work. As she finished a page, she passed it to Henry to read. "Come join us, Jane," she said.

I was a little afraid to; I thought I might reveal that I wasn't as smart as Julia might think. But I took the seat next to Henry, and read his discard pile.

I liked the pages I read, about a girl whose parents were getting divorced; it was more real than I would've expected.

When I looked up, my parents were watching the three of us and smiling.

I told Julia how much I liked the book and it made her really excited. Mostly she edited children's books, but she was starting to publish ones for my age group, which she called YA, or young adult.

Once my parents were out of earshot, I admitted that I hardly went to the library, and when I did I asked the librarian for books that she felt would be inappropriate for my age.

I told Julia that novels for my age group always seemed to be about what your life was supposed to be like, instead of what it was. Same with magazines. "Even the ads are false," I said. "Like they'll show a boy picking up a girl for a date with a handful of daisies behind his back. Nobody my age goes on dates. The word 'date' is not even in my vocabulary."

Julia was so interested that I was tempted to tell her about The House, the abandoned shack by the railroad tracks where kids went to get high and make out. I'd only gone there once, when a boy I liked casually mentioned that he'd be there.

When I walked in, he said, "Hey." I smoked a cigarette and tried to act like I belonged there. He came over and sat with me on the ripped sofa. He passed me the bong. I shook my head, and smiled as though I was already really high. Then he leaned over, just as I'd wanted him to. But he whispered, "Are you horny?"—the opposite of a sweet nothing.

———•———

They had other places to go—Julia had friends in Amagansett and Fire Island—and the weekend they went up to Martha's Vineyard, I brought Linda to the shore. We slept in the lower bunks. When I told her about Julia sneaking into Henry's room, she asked if I thought they had sex in there.

I heard my father's voice coming from my parents' bedroom and wondered if they could hear me. I whispered, "Can you have sex without making any noise?"

"Who knows?" she said.

I thought of the words Julia used, and imitated her breathing heavily and saying, "Exquisite. Extraordinary. You're no octogenarian, Hank." We laughed, but right afterward, trying to fall asleep, I felt terrible.

———•———

On the beach, Linda became her social-scientist self and said, "At the top of the social hierarchy is the blond man on the elevated white chair. The symbolic throne."

"I believe the common term 'lifeguard' signifies his desire to copulate," I said, "i.e., to guard the perpetuation of the species."

"Note that he paints his nose white," she said. "Not unlike the chiefs of many sub-Saharan tribes."

The lifeguard stood up and blew his whistle.

I said, "Mating call."

———•———

My parents loved Linda. That night, when we said we were going to see the moon on the ocean, they said, "Fine," in unison, even though it was late. Once we were out the door, I imitated myself saying, "We're going to rob a liquor store!" and my parents saying, "Fine!"

On the beach, there was a big crowd sitting around a

bonfire, and my fearless friend walked right up and sat down in the circle. I sort of followed her.

There was a keg, but when someone asked if we'd like a beer, Linda said, "I wish we could." I didn't find out what she'd meant until a joint was passed to her and she handed it right off to me, saying, "Remember the three Ds from detox: don't, don't, don't."

I passed the joint, as though exerting heroic self-control.

She said, "You still get flashbacks?"

"I think I always will," I said.

"Remember," she said, "never say 'always.' "

"I really appreciate your support," I said.

She said, "It helps me stay strong."

I said, "Every day is a gift."

—•—

Linda's parents were taking her to Disney World, against her wishes, but she came to the shore one last time. That was the weekend we saw the house going up across the lagoon, in the vacant lot that had given us our bay view. I woke up to hammering and rock music. Linda was still sleeping.

I went out to the porch, where my father was standing in his tennis clothes, white shorts and a white polo shirt but no socks, as though the sight of the workmen had upset him too much to continue getting dressed.

The frame for the house was already up—brand-new orange wood beams obscuring the view they'd soon completely block. I put my arm around his back, which was what he did with me when I was upset. "We'll be able to look right in their windows," I said brightly. "It'll be great."

He kissed the top of my head.

My mother said, "Julie and Henry should be here when you get back from tennis."

"Jul*ia*," he said. My mother's trouble with names was a standard joke between them, like an old song, and he said the refrain: "What's the plumber's name, Lou?"

"Pete McDaniel?" she said, smiling.

"Dan McGavin," he said, shaking his head. I was relieved to hear my dad laugh, though I thought they were past due for new jokes.

———•———

Julia and Henry showed up at the beach after lunch. When I introduced Linda, my brother's expression reminded me how pretty she was, and for a second I wished that I hadn't brought her.

She was as good at riding waves as Henry, and they stayed in the ocean a long time.

I went in the water and out. Julia sat under the umbrella, knitting a sweater. It was beautiful—a creamy turtleneck—and other times when I'd seen her work on it, I wondered if we'd ever be close enough for her to knit one for me. But now I worried that knitting might make her look older to Henry. My grandmothers knitted.

She and Henry left to see if my father had bought the boat he'd been considering. After they'd gone, Linda put on her social-scientist voice and said, "A form of nest-building, knitting signals readiness to mate."

"Please don't say that," I said. "I like her."

—•—

My father had bought the sailboat, and back at the house, Henry asked if Linda and I wanted to try it out.

He'd sailed before, on Nantucket, but Julia was a better sailor by a million knots. She moved around the boat as though she'd sailed all her life, and she probably had.

We had to tack out of the lagoon. She told us to come about, and then when she said, "Hard a-lee," Henry imitated her and laughed. It reminded me of my father kidding my mother, except Julia didn't seem to like it and that didn't make Henry stop.

It almost hurt not to laugh along with my brother, but I didn't, and neither did Linda.

—•—

Before dinner, while Linda showered outside and Julia inside, Henry and I sat on the porch, waiting for our turns. The house across the lagoon had walls now, and we couldn't see the sunset on the bay. Still, it was the end of the day, the only time here that reminded me of Nantucket. The light was warm and pink, and made the trees and water look soft—it was like seeing everything through a fond memory.

I asked Henry if they'd had a good time on Martha's Vineyard.

He said, "It was okay." He told me they'd stayed at the

youth hostel, as though this explained something, and I waited to hear what.

Then he told me he'd decided to start Columbia in the fall. He said it importantly, and I wondered if he thought starting school meant breaking up with Julia. Maybe he was already seeing himself on campus, and thinking she wouldn't fit in.

I said, "You'll still be in New York."

He nodded.

My father was glad, of course. He probably wouldn't relax about it for a while, though, maybe not until he actually saw Henry in a gown and mortarboard.

———•———

Labor Day weekend, Henry and Julia went to Southampton for her mother's big party. My parents had one to go to, too, and that night, walking Atlas, I heard parties on both sides of the lagoon. I thought that Oliver Biddle and I were probably the only ones who hadn't been invited to any. To cheer myself up, I said to Atlas, "It's just you and me, Pepper."

———•———

My grandmother came down on Sunday. It was raining, which affected her arthritis and made her even crankier than usual. She asked questions like, *Louise, why are you wearing those shorts?*

My father retreated to the bedroom for a nap.

When she said her standard, "Remember the haircut you got in Paris that spring?" referring to my mother's junior year abroad, twenty-five springs ago, my mother faked a yawn and said she was going to take a nap.

Once my grandmother and I were alone, I said, "I think my mom likes her hair now."

"It looked better then," my grandmother said.

I said, "How would you feel if you liked your hair short, and your mother kept telling you it looked better long?"

"I'd wear it long if I could," she said. Then she turned on me. "You should brush your hair, Jane," she said. "You might be pretty if you tried."

I didn't even fake a yawn, just went into my parents' room. They were reading in bed, and I got in the middle.

"She's obsessed with that Paris haircut," I said. "What did it look like, anyway?"

"I have no idea," my mother said.

"She's obsessed with hair, period," I said, though my parents seemed to be reading instead of listening. I told them my grandmother seemed to believe that the window of the soul was hair, instead of eyes.

My mother giggled. Around her mother, she became my age.

My father said, "Hair is the roof of the soul."

—•—

Before dinner, my grandmother read the newspaper, tsk ing and complaining to no one in particular that the world was going to hell. Everything was wrong; nothing was the way it used to be.

"What do you think was so good about the good old days?" I asked, in exasperation. But I heard how harsh my voice was and didn't like it. I said, "What do you miss, I mean?"

While she thought, I waited to make my point: that everything was much better now than it used to be; I'd cite the civil rights and women's movements.

"The boy who lit the street lamps in the evening," she said, finally. "He carried a stool with him."

I understood then—it was like missing Nantucket—and I put my hand on top of hers. It occurred to me that everything was more complicated than I thought.

———•———

We were finishing dessert when Henry and Julia showed up.

Right away, my mother acted like we were all in on a big surprise for my grandmother—*Look! Here's Henry!* He didn't even seem to notice. He let my mother introduce Julia, who was trying to smile and not quite pulling it off.

Maybe my grandmother could see Julia was older, or she might've disapproved of any girlfriend Henry brought home; she gave him a big hug—like he was still a boy and still belonged to us—and gave Julia an Ice Queen, "How do you do?"

Henry sat in the farthest seat from Julia's. He didn't look at her, and a few minutes later he went to his room.

I waited a while for him to come out, and when

he didn't I went in after him. "What are you doing?" I asked.

He didn't answer. He was holding his guitar, but just moving his fingers around to make chords he didn't play.

"Julia is out there alone," I said. "With Grandmom."

"She can take care of herself," he said.

I said, "She shouldn't have to take care of herself," and went back to the kitchen.

My grandmother had started doing the dishes. I told her I'd do them, but she just moved over. I rinsed the plates and handed them to her to put in the dishwasher.

She kept handing plates back to me to rerinse. "You're not washing them thoroughly," she said.

"I'm just rinsing them," I said. "The dishwasher is supposed to wash them. That's why it's called a *dishwasher.*"

My father gave me a stern look.

I was ready to abandon my post at the sink, but I stayed where I was for Julia's sake. I was her shield.

I imagined that we were in wartime Paris, and my job was to distract the Nazi hausfrau from Julia, the Jewish woman we were hiding until she could escape; I was her only chance.

It was my parents who escaped, to their room, though it wasn't even ten o'clock.

Julia was just waiting to go into Henry's room to talk. But I knew my grandmother would stay up as long as we did. When I suggested a walk to Julia, my grandmother protested, but we left anyway.

In the driveway, Julia said, "I could use a drink."

I told her I knew somewhere we could go.

"Just a guess," she said, "but I don't think your parents would want me to take you to a bar."

"That's true," I said. "It's not just a bar, though."

I ran back inside and asked Henry for the keys to his convertible. I said, "Julia and I are going out drinking and to meet men."

He just pointed to the keys on his bureau.

It had stopped raining, and Julia put the top down, which made me feel like we were embarking on Julia and Jane's Great Adventure, but I looked over at her and saw the grim line her mouth made. She pulled a chiffony scarf out of the glove compartment and wrapped it over her hair and twice around her neck, movie-star style. I wondered how she did it, and I decided I'd ask her to show me sometime when she wasn't upset.

When we got to the restaurant, I took out my pack of cigarettes, and she asked if she could have one. But she looked guilty, like it was her fault that I was smoking in the first place.

After she ordered her glass of wine and was sipping it, I asked her what had happened.

"I wish I knew," she said. "It was a huge party," she said. Everyone was there, her whole family and all of their lifelong friends. "Hank didn't seem to like anyone, though," she said.

She said that maybe it was hard for him to meet her family. "My family isn't like yours," she said; everyone had been divorced at least once, and there were half brothers and half sisters and step-everythings. She said that her parents had gotten divorced and then married each other again, which reminded me of Henry transferring back and forth to Brown.

She said, "They're always on the verge of splitting up or getting back together."

"Was it always like that?"

"The first time my mother left I was younger than you are," she said. "We'd just moved to Connecticut, into this nice house. It had a pool that was painted black, and the lights had been hung in such a way that the trees reflected on the water. When my parents gave parties, I'd watch from my bedroom window. It looked as though the guests were swimming through an underwater forest."

"It sounds beautiful," I said.

"Magic." She looked at my cigarettes, asking if I minded if she took another, and I nodded, *Go ahead.*

"It was September when Mom left. At night Dad used to go down to the pool and swim laps, even once it got cold. The pool was covered with leaves, but he swam right through them. I'd stand at the edge trying to talk him out of the water. By the time he did get out, there was a cleared path in the middle of the pool, and I could see the reflection of the bare branches on the water."

Then she was quiet. She wasn't crying, but she kept on covering her eyes with her hand like she might.

I thought she was upset about her parents all over again, plus Henry. So, I told her all of the nice things my brother had said about her, every compliment I could remember, and every comment that could be interpreted as a compliment. Then I listed all of her positive traits, and all the things I'd seen her do well.

"It doesn't work like that," she said, and I was hoping she would tell me how it did work.

Maybe she could see that, because she went on. "Sometimes you're loved because of your weaknesses," she said. "What you can't do is sometimes more compelling than what you can."

For a second, I felt hope for myself. But loving for weaknesses seemed like a weakness itself. "I think Henry does love you," I said, and then realized that I didn't know. "How could he not?"

She looked tired.

I told her the truth, that he was different with her than with other girlfriends he'd brought home. With them, he'd acted like they just happened to be there. As I said it, though, I remembered him not sitting with her at dessert. That was how he'd been with girlfriends before.

She looked right at me. "He doesn't say he loves me."

She seemed to be asking if Henry had told me he loved her—which made me feel even worse for her. "Did you ever tell him?" I said, and wondered at my advicey tone. I was acting like I knew something when I didn't— maybe like I knew Henry well enough to tell her what to do about him.

But her face smoothed out and looked new again, and she was nodding, like maybe I had a point.

I tried to go backward and talk about what I did know. I told her about one girl he'd brought home from Cornell; I'd asked if she was his girlfriend, and he'd said, "When you define something, you limit it."

Julia smiled, as though she could feel sorry for this other girl.

Everything I said now seemed to assure her that her problems with Henry were minor, and I worried that they weren't. Finally, I said, "If it doesn't work out with Henry, there's always Cinders."

She laughed and said that Cinders had been dead for years.

"Well," I said, "there are plenty of other horses."

———•———

When we got back to the house, only the hall light was on, and Julia said, "I'm going to talk to Henry for a little while."

"Good luck," I said, and just as I did, my grandmother came into the hall, so Julia was forced to stay in the manless land of bunk beds with us.

———•———

I woke up late. My grandmother had already left. "She didn't want to wake you," my mother said. "She had a party to go to in Philadelphia."

"She's a party animal," I said.

My mother smiled. "I wish you'd seen how pretty she looked."

It made me remember my grandmother saying that I might be pretty if I tried. I hadn't told my mother, but I still felt betrayed by her spirit of forgiveness. I said, "Isn't beauty an accident, Mom?"

"She puts herself together so well, though," my mother said, and went on to describe the knife-pleat skirt, high heels, and white gloves her mother had worn.

I let her finish. Then I asked where Henry and Julia were. They'd just left to play tennis, my mother said. "Why don't you get your racket and join them?"

I was surprised that they were playing tennis instead of talking about their problems. But maybe they had already talked. Maybe everything was fine now.

In case it was, I put my racket in my bike basket and rode over to the courts.

They were still warming up and didn't see me. Julia was wearing a tennis dress and looked clean and tanned. Henry had on cutoffs and high-tops, which you weren't supposed to wear on the courts.

"Let's play," my brother said.

Julia spun her racket. I heard her say, "Rough or smooth?"

He said, "Rough," like it was a joke.

Then they saw me, and Henry said, "You want to play?"

I said that I wanted to watch.

It was Julia's serve. She had beautiful form—I could see years of lessons in every stroke. Henry had taught himself how to play and was just batting the ball back however he could—backhand, forehand, or in-between hand if he had to, he didn't care. His shots were either impossible to return or way out—one ball went over the fence and all the way into the lagoon.

He lost that first game, and she went up to the net.

He said, "What?"

She said, "We switch sides."

"Okay," he said.

As they passed each other, he tapped her butt with his racket, just softly, but it didn't seem affectionate.

He'd never learned to hold two balls at once, and he put one behind him, at his feet. He had a hilarious serve—he bent his knees and swung his racket back at the same time. But the serve was strong, and Julia had trouble returning it.

He won that game and walked up to the net, without collecting the balls for her.

"We don't switch sides," she said.

"I thought you just said we did."

"On odd games," she said.

The rules weren't new to Henry, and I stared at him. I didn't know what he was doing, but I didn't want to watch.

I said, "You guys look good out there."

Julia asked if I wanted to take her place, but I thanked her anyway, and got on my bike.

At home, my father was reading a book she had given him.

"Is that good?" I asked.

He said, "Very good."

He asked how tennis was, and I told him that Julia was a beautiful player.

"How'd Henry do?"

I imitated Henry's serve, and my dad laughed.

Then, I said, "Something's wrong between them."

"That happens," he said. He wasn't dismissing me; he was saying that their problems didn't belong to us.

I looked across the lagoon at the new house. It was almost finished. It had gone up incredibly fast—with spit and Scotch tape, my father said—and it was huge and reminded me of a Walt Disney cartoon of a rich person's house, with columns and an elaborate roof that swooped like a water slide. I called it the Splash Palace.

It made me sad to look at it, and I said to my father, "Do you think we'll ever go back to Nantucket as a family?"

"I don't know, love," he said.

Then he asked what I missed about Nantucket. It was different from how he usually talked to me; if I had a problem, he would try to help me solve it. But I remembered our last Nantucket debate, and I wasn't sure it was safe to say how I really felt.

Even so, I tried to tell him. I felt things I couldn't say— they had to do with the sunlight filtering through the big old leafy trees and the mist on the cobblestones at night— and named the things I could: the band concerts we'd go to on Straight Wharf, the silent movies at the church, the whaling museum on rainy days. As I spoke, though, I realized that we hadn't done those things the last summer we'd been there. I worried that maybe what I missed most I'd never have again, on Nantucket or anywhere.

"What else?" he said, and his voice was so nice I felt like crying, and then I was. He handed me his hand-kerchief, which smelled of the pipe tobacco he kept in a pouch in his back pocket. "What else?" he said again.

I told him I missed looking at the stars from the Maria Mitchell Observatory and fishing at Hummock Pond.

When I said, "Swimming lessons at Children's Beach," he laughed because I'd complained about them so bit-terly. To acknowledge my fortitude, he'd taken me out to dinner at the end of each summer, just the two of us. He asked if I remembered our first dinner, at Vincent's, and I nodded. He said that I'd brought the card certifying me as an advanced beginner and shown it to the waiter.

I gave his handkerchief back to him.

Then he said, "Want to go out to lunch with me now?" And we went.

———•———

So, I didn't get to say good-bye to Julia. On the mail ta-ble, I found a package she'd sent to my mother. The card was a watercolor of a sailboat. Although the note began "Dear Louise," I read it to to see if there was anything about Henry. Or me. But she'd just written about sailing and the beach, and how much she'd enjoyed getting to know us—until the P.S.: "The enclosed is for Jane."

It was wrapped like a present—way too small for the

sweater I'd hoped for—but I was thrilled. She'd given me a copy of *The Great Gatsby* and written a single line on the flyleaf: "This seems inappropriate for your age."

—•—

I knew that Julia and Henry had broken up, but I thought maybe they'd get back together, like her parents. I was hoping she'd come to the shore with Henry as a surprise. Just in case, I brought my best drawing to show her.

But Henry arrived alone. He'd shaved. You could see the slightest bit of paleness where his beard had been. Otherwise, his face was the same as always. Still, I had trouble getting used to it.

No one mentioned Julia.

I went back into my bedroom and looked at the drawing again, critically, as though her not showing up proved it wasn't good. It was like all my others—just people standing around. I'd never be able to illustrate a children's book, I decided, unless there was one about loitering.

—•—

It was warm on the beach. Indian summer. Henry told me that he'd started to write a novel.

"Maybe Julia could help," I said. "She edits children's books."

I could see how hurt he was, and I apologized. But I told him that I liked Julia, and I wanted to know why they'd broken up.

He didn't answer right away. Then he told me about the gala in Southampton. The house was enormous, he said, and right on the beach. There were at least a hundred guests—maybe two hundred—and a band had been hired for the party.

He said that Julia had probably told him to wear a dark suit, but he'd forgotten or thought it wasn't important. They'd had to borrow one for him. He imitated her father saying, "All Blaire has to do is get on the horn." Henry seemed to dislike her father especially.

Henry described the borrowed suit in detail—the sleeves were too short, and it was baggy—but everyone told him how wonderful he looked. Other men were wearing tuxedos.

Everyone was drinking a lot, he said, and he drank, too. Julia kept introducing him to people, but Henry said he couldn't remember their names, and they didn't seem to want to talk to him anyway. He'd made jokes—about why he'd transferred to so many colleges, for example— but nobody laughed. When Julia asked him to dance with her, he said that you weren't supposed to dance to jazz. But he just didn't know how.

There were a lot of people Julia hadn't seen in a long time. They all wanted to talk to her. And dance. So, off she went.

He went to the bar and stood there a while. But he was in the way of people getting their drinks. He moved to the edge of the crowd and just watched. Suddenly it seemed, he was drunk, in a suit that didn't fit, at a party where he didn't know anyone, and he was standing alone.

I knew how I felt at parties. The worst thing was to get caught standing alone; it seemed to prove that you weren't worth talking to. I realized that it must have been even harder for him, because Julia had seen.

Still, he seemed to blame it all on her. Not in words— there was nothing I could point to or ask him about it.

I could see how hard it was for him to tell me, and I tried to be gentle when I said, "But that was just a bad party."

He didn't answer. I started to say, *Didn't you love her?* but I remembered Julia saying, *He doesn't say he loves me.* Instead, I said, "I thought you really liked her."

"I did," he said. "Julia's great."

"I loved her," I said.

He nodded. Then he said, "There was too much of an age difference."

It sounded to me like "better course selection," and I gave him a look to say so, but he pretended not to see.

—•—

At dinner, he ate his corn typewriter-style and told us funny stories about New York. He'd gone out with a dancer from the Midwest. He said that when she'd first arrived in New York, the dope dealers around Washington Square had said, "Loose joints, loose joints," and she'd said, "Thank you."

After dinner, he stayed out on the porch and talked to my father about the courses he was taking and which credits would transfer from the other colleges. He said that he was going to graduate from Columbia, and my father said, "Good."

My mother and I were clearing the dishes, and she

smiled when she heard that. She was caught up in our being together. It was a celebration. And when she said to me, "What's wrong?" it was in part a reprimand.

—•—

That night, alone with all those empty beds, I couldn't fall asleep. I got up and went outside to the dock in my nightgown. I'd finished *Gatsby,* and I looked out at the lagoon, hoping to see a green light. But nobody's dock was lit up. Only one house had any lights on, and the light was just the blue of a television set.

I tried to understand what Henry had told me. But I worried about that, too. Other people might not try as hard as I did to understand him. I was always on his side, no matter what. My parents were, too. All he really had to do with us was show up. More had been expected of him as Julia's boyfriend and at that party. More would be expected of him everywhere. I didn't know what had happened between him and Julia. It scared me to think that my brother had failed at loving someone. I had no idea myself how to do it.

THE
FLOATING
HOUSE

Insisting on playing a game for which, after a fair amount of time, you show no natural aptitude is frustrating to you and annoying to all but the most complacent opponents.

—From *Amy Vanderbilt's Book of Etiquette: A Guide to Gracious Living*

It's the morning of our flight. Jamie sets my coffee and his on the night table and gets back into bed with me. This afternoon we'll be in St. Croix, the guests of Jamie's ex-girlfriend and her new husband. Now I sit up and, without giving myself the go-ahead, speak. "Honey," I say, "I suddenly have a weird feeling about this trip."

He looks over at me.

I try to think of how to say it. "I don't know these people."

He says, "You'll be with me."

Jamie has a beautiful voice, deep and private, and it stops me for a moment. Then I say, "It just seems awkward. Going on vacation with your boyfriend's ex-girlfriend."

He tells me that he doesn't think of Bella that way, she's just an old friend now.

I say, "What does your old friend Bella look like?"

He laughs and pulls me in for a kiss. "It was college,"

he says, pronouncing *college* the way I now pronounce *high school.*

While he takes his shower, I watch him through the clear parts, the oceans, of his world-map shower curtain.

When he gets out he says, "Trust me."

———•———

From New York to San Juan, Jamie sleeps. I take off his baseball cap and touch his hair, which goes back behind his ears and flips up. He wears a white T-shirt, old jeans, and sneakers. He is long and lean, all legs, like a colt.

Jamie is my first real boyfriend.

We are three months old.

For me, it started the night he told me he couldn't sleep with a woman unless he really loved her.

"I'm monogamous by nature," he said.

I said, "Same here."

———•———

We land in St. Croix and walk off the plane into a tiny airport. I see a man holding up a sign that says JANE AND JAMES, and I'm thinking, *They sent a car for us?* But Jamie laughs and says, "There they are."

Bella is turn-and-stare gorgeous—big dark eyes, long dark hair, smooth dark skin.

She says, "James," which sounds like "gems," and kisses him—cheek, cheek, cheek.

The man I thought was the driver introduces himself as Yves, Bella's husband, and when he cheek-cheeks me, I think, *Grandmother, what soft lips you have.*

Bella takes both my hands in hers, as though she has been waiting a long time to meet me. She says, "Janie," my childhood nickname, and I am so thrown off by her warmth that I say, "Belly."

For a moment I hope no one has heard, but, leading us out to their jeep, Yves whispers to me, "It's *Bella.*"

The ride home is all wind. Jamie leans forward, in the space between the front seats, to talk to Bella.

When we pull up to the driveway, she jumps out of the jeep to unlatch the gate. First, though, she motions sweepingly to the sign on the wall, THE FLOATING HOUSE. Jamie squeezes my hand. I begin a joke about having known only generic houses, but the jeep lurches forward into the walled courtyard.

The house is cool and long, white ceramic tiled floors out to the veranda, and from every window you can see the blue-green Caribbean Sea.

Bella shows us the view from our room. When she speaks her voice is an orgy of accents. "My stepfather is the *arr*-she-tekk," she tells us. "He designed the windows so you feel the water. You will see," she says, "the house is cool." Her vowels and consonants are all off—trying to understand her is like picking fish out of the clover and goats from the ocean.

Yves fixes us drinks, rum and whatever we want, and carries the tray out to the veranda. Below, the yard is long and steep, bordered by flowering trees down to the dock.

Bella says to Jamie, "Alessandra sends you all her love."

While Yves asks me about the flight, the snow, the bracelet I am wearing, I overhear Belly telling Gems about close friends he's never mentioned who live all over the world. It occurs to me that all my close friends live in the tristate area.

"Can we swim down there?" Jamie asks her.

"Of course," she says.

Jamie turns to me and says, "Let's go swimming," like he's eleven, which I love.

We change into our bathing suits, both of us pale as larvae, and then we walk down to the water. As soon as I go under, I begin to feel like it's all going to be fine, wonderful, perfect. The water is turquoise and soft, and Jamie and I are somehow Jamie and me again. Then I look up and see Yves and Bella at the railing of the veranda, holding hands. When they wave to us it is like seeing a photograph move. I say this to Jamie and he tells me I've been reading too many South American novels, too much magical realism.

"That's not what I mean," I say.

"What then?"

"It has something to do with photorealism," I say.

"Painting," he says.

I realize that all I mean is that they seem posed, but I continue, bringing in the colors of the lawn leading up to the veranda, the brushstroke-like swirls on the pillars, anything to keep from sounding as though I'm criticizing his friends.

———•———

For dinner we have local lobster and eat on the veranda. Bella and Yves speak to each other almost entirely in French. At first, Jamie interjects stray French phrases, as though joking, but Yves says, "You speak very well," and soon Jamie does, with an ease that surprises me.

I have not spoken French since eighth grade, when I learned about a wholesome French family living on the third floor of an apartment building near the railroad station. I remember that sometimes they took the elevator, sometimes the stairs.

"We visited Yves's parents at Christmas," Bella says, in English, touching Yves's cheek with the back of her hand. "They are so nice."

To me, she says, "How is your lobsters?"

"Nice," I say, realizing only afterward that I've mimicked her, a bad habit of mine; I'm like one of those animals that imitates its predators to survive.

———•———

In bed, Jamie says, "How do you like Bella?"

A voice tells me to say, *Great,* and I obey.

He smiles. "I thought you'd like her."

I say, "I myself have dated several mannequins."

"Honey," he says, and reminds me that Bella is a good friend of his. I should give her a chance.

Here in the dark, I mouth, *You're right, I'm sorry.*

By the time I get the sound to come out, he's asleep.

———•———

We drive through the hills on the ocean side. I sit up front with Yves. I keep seeing animals that look like bushy-tailed rats scurrying across the road. He tells me they're mongeese. "They were imported at the turn of the century from India," he says, "to kill the snakes. And they did. They killed the snakes, and today . . ." He takes his hands off the wheel and motions for me to finish the story.

"And today," I say, "the island is overrun with mongeese."

He smiles at me and tells me that boys trap them for fifty cents a tail.

We park when the road ends. Now I see how dry it is, the bald spots; what I thought were trees are cacti. Yves has prepared a picnic lunch. The beer and sun make me sleep, and I wake up to Yves rubbing lotion on my back.

"You are burning," he says.

Jamie is in the water. I stand up to join him, but then Bella surfaces. They're laughing. Ha, ha, ha, ho, ho, ho.

—•—

After showers, we're changing for dinner.

"You know," I say, "I think it would be easier if I spoke French."

"You probably could," Jamie says, "if you let yourself."

"Excuse me?"

"It's like Shakespeare—after a certain point, it just comes over you."

At dinner, I try to let it come over me.

Bella speaks, and I translate: *Gems, you silly boy, you want to touch my breasts, is it not so?*

———•———

Jamie is gone when I wake up.

The sky is white.

On the veranda, Yves rises when he sees me and gets me a cup of coffee.

I ask where Jamie is.

Yves says, "Maybe they went for a walk."

I go swimming. I take a shower. I read.

"The day isn't good," he says. He suggests we go into town.

I watch Yves as he drives. He has nice crow's-feet. I realize how soft he is, how unaffectedly feminine, like a boy raised by his older sisters.

He asks me questions about my job in publishing. I tell him I'm an editorial assistant, really just a secretary, but I get to read unsolicited manuscripts.

He tells me that he's written a novel.

I ask him what it's about, and he says, "The human art," or "The human heart"—I can't hear him above the wind—but he looks at me as though we two understand each other, and I nod as though we two do.

In Christiansted, Yves leads me through the court-yards of old fortresses and along the docks. He points his toe a little when he walks, like Marcel Marceau.

He takes me into a huge duty-free shop that sells perfume, china, crystal, and watches. He sprays perfume on me, smells it, and gives the verdict—"Sweet," "Musky," "Clean"—before I sniff. When we've used up my wrists and arms, he chooses one and buys it for me.

Outside it's raining. He puts his arm around me and shuttles me into a restaurant on the dock.

The waitress, blonde and Southern, says to him, "Where you been?"

"Resting," he says.

Before we leave, he goes over and speaks to her.

——•——

When we get home, Bella turns her head slowly and looks at Yves.

He says, "We had lunch in town."

Bella answers in French.

Jamie asks if I want to go for a swim.

"So," I say, once we're in the water, "where'd you go this morning?"

"Just for a walk," he says.

"Oh," I say. "I saw some old fortresses."

I realize we sound like strangers who happen to be staying at the same hotel. But he's waiting for me to finish, so I say, "They were big."

——•——

That night, we all drive back to Christiansted. Bella stops in front of the restaurant with the Southern waitress, but Yves suggests another, and we go to a bar with tables on the dock.

Jamie tells them about the restaurant he'd like to open and then the screenplay he plans to write, and Bella listens, leaning forward, watching his face.

"So what do you guys do?" I ask after my second drink.

Bella says, "We are just here until my stepfather sells the house."

"How is Alberto?" Jamie asks Bella.

I ask Yves, "What do you do?"

Bella stops talking and turns to listen.

"What do I do?" Yves says. "Take pictures. Write novels. Play the piano."

I say, "I didn't see a piano."

He tells me that Europeans are different from Americans—not so single-minded about careers. "The most important thing is to live freely."

I say, "Live free or die, I guess."

———•———

Back at the house, I smoke a cigarette on the veranda before going to bed.

Yves comes out. "Jane?" he says, and kisses my cheek so slowly it's like his lips are melting onto my skin. "Good night."

In the bedroom I ask Jamie, "What's going on?"

"What do you mean?" He's almost asleep.

"Well, something is."

He doesn't answer. I wonder if it is because he doesn't know.

———•———

In the shower, I say, "I was just noticing how we don't have sex anymore."

Jamie looks at me like I'm fully clothed.

I say, "Why did you and Bella ever break up, anyway?"

He doesn't answer right away. "She slept with some-one else."

"Oh," I say.

He says, "She wanted to make me jealous."

I say, "Is that what she's doing now?"

"Why would she want to make me jealous?"

I stare at him. "I meant *Yves.*"

"What are you talking about?" he says, and gets out of the shower.

I turn off the water and follow him, even though I still have shampoo in my hair.

I wrap myself in a towel and watch him smear a patch of the steamed mirror to shave.

I am trembling a little when I say, "I want you to stop this thing with Bella."

He tells me I've got it all wrong, she needs to talk to him about her problems with Yves.

I say, "How about if she talks to Yves about her prob-lems with Yves?"

He turns around and says, "She doesn't trust him."

"So why'd she marry him?"

"It's sad," he says, and we are not arguing anymore, we are talking about a couple less fortunate than our-selves, and I believe him and trust him, and I let my towel drop and pull him toward me. I kiss his neck, his chest, his mouth.

There's a knock, and Bella says, "We have a court in fifteen minutes."

"Okay," Jamie calls back.

To me, he says, "Later."

———•———

We play tennis at a nearby hotel, and before anyone says anything, I insist on being Yves's partner. We are all strong players so it doesn't much matter who plays with whom, but I watch her face when I say it. She looks at me and I smile, *Hiya.*

I compliment Yves on his shots. He compliments me on mine. We have huddles. We have strategies. We have signs. Across the court, Bella begins to double-fault.

After tennis, we walk by the pool, and Bella kneels down as if to splash water on her face, but she splashes Jamie instead. He splashes her. It escalates until Jamie throws Bella into the pool.

The lifeguard blows his whistle.

Bella climbs up the ladder, her wet hair sticking to her head like a helmet. Of course you can see her breasts through her soaked white shirt.

"Now look what you did," she says to Jamie.

———•———

In the middle of the night, I wake up to Jamie's mouth on mine. I reach for the light, as is our custom, but he pulls my arm back around him.

———•———

Once Jamie is asleep, I go out to the living room. I light a cigarette and call my brother, who introduced me to Jamie.

Henry answers on the first ring and says, "Hey," as though he's been expecting my call.

I tell him about the house and the view, the mongeese. I am talking just to keep him on the phone, and he knows it. Finally, I tell him about Jamie throwing Bella in the pool.

Henry says, "I'm sure Jamie's totally oblivious."

"I don't think that's possible," I say.

"This is you," Henry says, softly but with authority.

We don't talk for a long moment.

"Well," I say, "I should get back to guarding the bedroom."

"Jamie would never do anything," Henry says.

I say, "I think he likes it, though."

"You can't really blame him for that," Henry says. He tells me that the best man I will ever find will be attracted to other women.

I hear this as another fact I am too old not to know. More proof of how unprepared I am to love anyone.

——•——

Clearing the breakfast dishes, Bella leans into Jamie.

In our bedroom, I say, "I think I would be more comfortable if Bella weren't always touching you."

"It's a European thing," he says.

"A European thing," I say.

——•——

In the late afternoon, I tell Yves I'd like to buy perfume for a friend. He drives me to town, but the store is closed.

Instead, we go to the bar with the tables on the dock. I try to ask him questions, but I see this is not how to talk to Yves.

"You are so young," he says, "even for your age." His tone is charmed and only half avuncular as he describes me to me.

I start telling the story I always tell, about my loving family and the principles I grew up with, but I surprise myself, and I say, "I was afraid of sex before Jamie."

I'm about to tell him more, but he touches my wrist, making a soft spiral.

I want him to, and what makes me pull my wrist back is not fear of sex or love for Jamie but the restraint self-righteousness requires.

———•———

After dinner, I volunteer to do the dishes. Yves clears. He sits on a stool, watching me scrape the plates into the garbage. I can feel his eyes on me.

"Could you not stare at me, please?" I say.

I hear Bella's voice: "Where are the cards?" she says. "We'll play some poker."

Yves sets up the bar on the veranda. Bella counts out our make-do poker chips, olives and sword-shaped plastic toothpicks.

I tell Yves that my grandparents taught me to play poker when I was little. "I think I learned the shtetl version, though," I say.

"Let's play," Bella says.

I say, "I'm not very good at cards."

"Poker's not really a card game," Jamie says. "It's a money-management game."

We each roll an olive to the center of the table. "Seven card stud, high-low?" Bella says. She deals each of us two cards face down and one card face up.

I say, "Can someone just tell me the rules of this money-management game?"

Yves says, "It goes one pair, two pairs, three of a kind—" He stops to look at his hand. "Straight, flush—"

"Jack bets," Bella says.

"It's a mind game," Jamie says, betting an olive.

The game changes with each dealer, and I give up trying to learn. Instead, I decide to be The Big Loser, a playboy in an ascot, jumping trains to escape creditors. I raise everyone, not with olives, but swords. On Yves's deal, he shows surprise that I'm folding, but I mouth, "Nothing," about the cards he can't see, and I give a Lady-Luck-isn't-smiling-on-me shrug.

It's hotter than it's been. It's less like the end of spring and more like the middle of summer. Bella changes into a black sleeveless dress that looks like a wetsuit. Yves, forever freshening our drinks, carries his cards to and from the bar, sometimes in his shirt pocket. Jamie's little array of booty is growing, mainly because whenever Bella folds, she nuzzles over and plays his hand with him. I tell myself that I can quit as soon as I lose everything, and to this end I begin eating my olives.

Bella turns to me and says, "You are bored with the game."

"Me?" I say.

"We could change it," she says, shuffling. "Would you like to change it?"

"Sure."

"Well, strip poker then." She says, "Five card draw, no high-low," and deals.

"Look," I say, "you don't have to change the game for me."

"No," she says. "You were right. The game was not interesting."

Yves takes my glass.

I look at Jamie, *Hi, Jamie, it's me, Jane.*

He looks at me, but he doesn't know himself what his look says.

I try to remember crisis advice I've heard: From my mother, on boys out of control, *Call us and we'll come get you;* from my high-school gym teacher, on averting rape, *Go down on all fours and eat grass.*

The first few hands, I fold without betting. Yves wins, Jamie wins, and Yves again. Then I get three aces. I bet and win. Yves passes me Jamie's watch; Jamie slides me Yves's shirt, which is white-and-yellow striped, cotton so fine it has a sheen to it. And Boom-Boom half rises and wriggles out of her wet suit, under which she wears nothing.

I can almost hear the voice in Jamie's head, to the rhythm of his accelerated heartbeat: *Don't look, don't look.*

I expected Bella's breasts to be round and perfect like in magazines, but they are just regular, not so different from mine.

Yves freshens our drinks.

Jamie stares at the cards he's already played.

Bella glances at him, and I suddenly see how angry she is. When Yves starts dealing the next hand, she pushes her cards back.

He collects all of our cards, shuffles, and starts a new deal, leaving her out.

She rises and walks unsteadily, as though in high heels, inside.

I keep waiting for Yves to follow her, but he doesn't.

I forget that I don't know how to play the game, and I stay in, betting and losing until I've got nothing but real clothes to bet with. Then, I say, "I'm out."

"You can't fold once someone is naked," Yves says. "I've got a full house." He turns my cards over. "A pair of tens."

I say, "Don't you think you should've told me the rules?"

Yves shrugs. "It's just a game."

I mean to say, *It's not a game,* but I wind up saying, "I'm not a game."

"Yves—" Jamie says in a voice I don't recognize—it may be the voice of a man starting a fight with a man.

Bella interrupts. "I think our guests are tired," she says from the other side of the screen door. The house is dark, and I can just make out her bathrobe.

Even when she slides open the door and comes out, Yves doesn't move. She stands beside him at the table, and then sweeps the swords into a pile. "We are all tired," she says.

"Here's what I want to know," I say to her. I am so nervous my voice comes out throaty.

"It's pretty obvious you wanted to sleep with Jamie to make Yves jealous," I say. "Right? I mean, even I can get that much."

Her look is so cold I almost stop.

"But then Yves goes after me—that's the part I don't get," I say. I can feel everyone not wanting me to speak. It is like fuel. "I mean, why would you want to watch that?"

Jamie is shaking his head.

Yves looks irritated.

Bella blinks, and I realize, *She didn't know.* And I suddenly imagine myself as her, hearing these questions put to me by a stranger.

—— • ——

Back in our room, I sit on the chair by the window while Jamie undresses and brushes his teeth.

He comes up behind me and bends down and kisses my neck.

I don't know what to do, so I talk.

I say, "Do you wish I hadn't said anything?"

He says, "I think Bella's in a lot of pain."

A moment later, he adds, "I don't think everything always has to be spelled out." There is an instructional quality to his voice that I haven't noticed before.

He kisses the top of my head. "Come to bed," he says.
I stay where I am.

The air is cooler now, with morning close. The sky is getting light. At this hour, you can believe that just staring at the stars will put them out.

I think about Jamie pretending that he was just being a good friend to Bella, who wasn't trying to seduce him, which was my delusion.

I get into bed, underpants on.

Jamie is still awake and trying hard to sleep, his head under the pillow, blocking out noise and light.

—•—

In the afternoon when I wake up, the Belladrama appears to be over. The three of them are on the veranda having breakfast. The sun is out and sparkling away on the water, and there's fruit salad and juice.

"Hi, babe," Jamie says.

"Hi," I say to the table at large.

I help myself to a bowl of fruit and walk around the table to the empty chair, past Jamie, who reaches for me as though we are a happy couple on a nice vacation.

"How did you sleep?" Yves asks, placing a cup of coffee in front of me.

"Okay," I say.

Yves says, "For your last day, we are thinking of renting a sailboat."

Bella says, "Do you like to sail?"

I don't answer right away.

"Henry's a big sailor," Jamie says, caulking over the silence. He adds, "Jane's brother. I can't remember if you ever met him," he says to Bella. "Henry Rosenal. Tall guy, glasses. He looks like Jane, only not pretty."

Everyone's looking at me; I have a new role here at the round table—She Who Must Be Appeased.

"At Columbia," she says. "We played tennis with him and Ramona at the court with all the rats."

"Right," Jamie says.

"He had a funny serve," she says, smiling at me.

Here we are on Day Six of our visit, having a Day One conversation. There's no evidence that anyone except me remembers Night Five. They're all wearing pokerless faces.

"I didn't meet Jane until last summer," Jamie says. "When I told Henry that I really liked her, he looked at me like, 'Keep your hands off my sister.' "

Yves laughs. Bella smiles. I eat their strawberries, raspberries, grapes, and bananas.

Jamie turns to me and suggests that just the two of us rent a sailboat. He says, "We haven't spent much time alone."

"That's true," I say.

Yves goes inside to call about a boat.

Jamie stacks the dishes on a tray and takes them inside. I hear him rinsing them for the dishwasher.

Which leaves Bella and me alone.

Looking out at the water, she says, "I have behaved badly. I am sorry for this."

I lift my head, neither accepting nor rejecting her apology.

"But it is not James's fault," she continues. "You should not punish him for the way I acted."

"At the moment," I say, "I'm trying not to punish *you* for the way *he* acted."

She raises her eyebrows, as though to say, *You are more interesting than I thought.* "But he did nothing. And he is the one you need to forgive," she says. "He is the one who matters—not me."

"Everyone matters," I say.

"You are making it harder than it has to be," she says.

I say, "And I should forgive him because it would be easier?"

"You don't need a reason to forgive," she says. "If you want to go on with someone, that is what you do."

I wonder if she knows more or less than I do. I say, "Well, I forgive you, Bella." And as soon as I say it, I do.

———•———

Yves drops us off at the docks and points to a sign for Cap'n Toby's Day Cruises, where we find a blond-bearded he-man heave-hoing a cooler onto the dinghy.

Jamie says, "Are you Cap'n Toby?"

"Tom, actually," he says. "James?" and the two shake hands.

I don't know why, but I instantly like this salty dog with his sunny hair and sunburnt tip o' nose. He is like a counselor and we are campers. "Chips ahoy," I say.

He chuckles and extends his huge blond-haired brown arm to me and helps me onto the little boat. He says, "Welcome aboard."

"Thanks, Cap'n," I say.

He motors us out to a huge beautiful sailboat, and the sight of it puts the wind back in my own sails. I see the boat's name, *The True Love*, and think of the one from *The Philadelphia Story*. To myself I say, "Yar," in my best Katharine Hepburn accent.

After Tom hauls the snorkeling gear and cooler and life preservers onto the deck, he asks if Jamie knows how to sail.

"Not really," he says.

You probably could if you let yourself, I think. *It's like Shakespeare—after a certain point, it just comes over you.*

Jamie says, "I've only sailed Sunfish."

It's a wind-management game, I think.

"Sorry," I say to Tom. "Landlubber."

Jamie says, "Can you sail it alone?"

"Not a problem," Tom says, and it isn't. He moves around the boat like the expert he is, and we're off. Tom works the sails, sometimes steering the wheel with one foot.

Jamie puts sunscreen on his legs and arms and chest, and hands it to me.

"No, thanks," I say.

I let the two of them go through the usual questions—where we're from, where he's from, where we're staying, why he stayed.

I go to the front of the boat, and stand in the wind. I do actually feel yar, as much from having the wind in my face as the Floating House at my back.

When we get near Buck Island, Tom drops the anchor and takes out masks and snorkels and flippers. I say that I've never snorkeled before.

He tells me I'll love it and takes my mask, which he spits into. Then he rinses it in the ocean water. "Cap'n," I say, "I can't believe you just spit in my mask."

He laughs. "Just how you clean it, matey," he says. And asks if we want to smoke a joint.

I say, "Are you going to spit on it?"

"Already did."

My own matey gives me a look.

"Better not," I say.

I climb down the ladder into the pale green water and under. I am amazed by the coral and sand and then I see my first fish. Yellow-and-white stripes! Then I see a school of blue ones. Then orange. They let me swim right up to them. I'm having such a good time, I laugh underwater, dancing in my fins. I am Flipper. I am in the undersea world of Jane Cousteau. I am hunting for treasure. Fending off sharks. I am Bond, Jane Bond.

But it's not easy for me to breathe through the snorkel, and I'm claustrophobic in the mask; I go up to the surface to demask and desnorkel. And then I see Jamie in his mask, and I bob and giggle, as he flippers over to me. He takes off his mask and snorkel and suggests we explore the island.

We walk in, now clumsy in our big-feet fins. "Wasn't that the coolest?" I say.

He says, "That was cool," but in his tone I think I hear the talk we are about to have, and I stop feeling so joyous.

At the shore, he says, "What the hell were you doing with that guy?"

I am stunned. "What are you talking about?"

"Flirting with that guy," he says.

"Cap'n Tom?" I say.

"I don't believe you," he says.

"I don't believe *you*," I say. But I feel like a fish clown in my flippers and have to take them off before I go on. "We're just friends," I say, mocking him. "Besides, I don't think everything needs to be spelled out."

"Okay," he says, "I get it."

"Good," I say. "Now multiply how you feel times six days and five nights."

"So, you're getting back at me," he says.

"No," I say, "I wasn't. I wasn't flirting with that guy. I just liked him."

We walk and walk. We are both fuming, which seems all wrong with the blue sky and green water. We pass another couple, holding hands. "Hey," they say, like we are four peas in a pod.

Jamie says a death-voiced "Hi" for both of us.

Then we're back at the beach where we started, facing the boat. Jamie sinks down in the sand, and I sink down beside him.

He turns to me. "I'm sorry," he says.

It's hard for him to apologize, and usually I just say, *Say no more* or *No prob* or *'Nuff said.* Now I say, "Tell me what you're sorry for, Jamie."

"I'm sorry I didn't listen to you," he says. "I'm sorry I put you through this."

"You left me stranded," I say, and my voice cracks.

"I know," he says, and I can hear that he does know and that he really is sorry.

It scares me how fast I go from disliking to loving him, and I wonder if it's this way for everyone.

Walking into the water, he asks me if I think Cap'n Tom is smoking a joint now.

"Probably," I say.

"And do you think we're going to capsize and drown?"

"Yes," I say. "We will swim with the fishies."

Pretending to be one, he comes at me, fluttering his fingers like fins. He gives me little fish kisses. Then we put our masks on, go under, and flipper out.

MY

OLD MAN

The only way for a woman, as for a man, to know herself as a person, is by creative work of her own.

—From *The Feminine Mystique* by Betty Friedan

Pin up on your bed, your mirror, your wall, a sign, lady, until you know it in every part of your being: *We were destined to delight, excite and satisfy the male of the species.*
Real women know this.

—From *The Sensuous Woman* by J

"Look up when you walk," my great-aunt Rita told me, the summer I stayed with her in Manhattan. "Tilt your chin," she said, lightly tapping her own. I was sixteen, and I listened to her because she was beautiful. She was tall for a woman, but small-boned, willowy, with long white hair she wore up in a chignon.

It was my last night with her, and we were going to the theater. I was already dressed in my Indian-print halter and wraparound skirt combo, and I lurked in the doorway to the bathroom, watching her put on the shade of red lipstick she'd told me Coco Chanel had invented. She noticed me then and looked me over, and her eyes paused at my Dr. Scholl's, the wood-heeled sandals that were the fad of my suburban high school.

Aunt Rita was cranky whenever it was humid or rainy, like my grandmother, her sister.

Following her into the bedroom, I heard my sandals clomp on the polished wood floor.

She shook her head.

I said, "They're all I have."

She handed me a pair of navy-blue pumps. They looked to me like shoes a stewardess would wear and were a size too small, but I squeezed into them. My feet began to hurt even before we left the apartment.

"That's better," my aunt said.

During the first act, she sat perfectly still and silent, enthralled.

At intermission, she went to the ladies' room to take her pill. She never took a pill in public. I was to wait for her in the lobby. My feet throbbed, and I shifted my weight, giving one foot a rest and then the other.

I scanned the crowd, thinking in placards: These Are the People Who Attend the Theater in Manhattan.

One older woman smiled over at me, spoke to her husband, and he turned to look in my direction, too. Then another woman did. I didn't really know what I looked like yet, and my face flushed with the possibility that I could be prettier here than at home.

Then I realized they were staring behind me, and I turned around to see.

You noticed her limbs first, long and tanned, and then her eyes and cheekbones and lips, perfect, like in magazines. She had on a hot-pink silk minidress with straps as thin as string. He was older, a big man, broad and tall, with blond hair and weathered skin. He wasn't handsome exactly, but his looks carried. He was teasing her, and she said something like, *Okay*, and she flexed her arm. He squeezed her biceps, and I saw, and faintly heard, him whistle. She laughed and he kept his hand there, around her beautiful arm.

When I spotted my aunt, I waved. She had on a fresh coat of Coco-red lipstick, and she seemed thrilled to see me. This was her party face. I knew because she'd told me. "When you're out," she'd advised, "try to appear captivated." It wasn't her fault; I begged her for tips.

She handed me a cigarette, lit mine and then hers. While she cataloged the flaws of the first act, I kept an eye on the famous couple, trying to learn something.

My aunt was asking me my opinion of the play.

"Good," I said.

" 'Good'?" my aunt said. "Children are *good*. Dogs are *good*. This is theater, Jane."

"Um," I said, and just as I was taking a last, loving look at the couple, the man caught me. I turned away fast, but I saw him say something to his girlfriend and head toward us.

"Oh," I said, and I heard the man's voice, like a growl, right beside me.

"Rita," he said.

She gave him her standard two cheek air kiss, but he said, "Nope."

He kissed my aunt right on the lips.

When she introduced me, I was too surprised to speak. After all, she was old enough to be his mother.

———•———

His name was Archie Knox, and my aunt liked him. That was rare. In the cab home, I asked her if he was famous.

"More famous than an editor should be," she said. "The best are invisible." She herself was a novelist.

"I bet his girlfriend is famous," I said. "A writer maybe. Or an actress. Somebody."

"No," my aunt said. "If she were, he would've brought her over."

"Archie Knox kissed you," I said.

She squeezed my hand and said, "Did you have a good time?"

When we got home, we took brandies out to her little terrace. There was a bigger one below us, and as we sat there, a couple came out and shared a cigarette. The woman stood against the wall, with her arms crossed.

"Who lives there?" I asked.

"Nina Solomon," she said. "She makes documentary films. Her husband is the painter Ben Solomon. If you were staying a little longer we could go to his gallery. And there's a book party I could take you to tomorrow night." She swirled her glass of brandy. "But literary people are so dull nowadays," she said. "I wish there were more Archie Knoxes."

I wanted to know about him, but I couldn't ask outright. "What did literary people used to be like?"

"They were Livers," she said. "Big livers."

I pictured the purplish-brown organ, and assumed she meant hard drinkers.

My aunt said, "Now all they do is talk."

———•———

After my freshman year in college, I spent a long weekend with my aunt on Martha's Vineyard. Late on a hazy afternoon, she took me to the clay baths. We walked down the beach, and as we neared the baths, I saw that everyone was naked, their clay-coated bodies varying shades of gray, depending on dryness. I looked over at my aunt.

She said, "A parade of statues," and I could tell by the way she said it—listening to herself—that she was testing the line for a novel.

I didn't feel young with her now so much as provincial. When we got to the clay pit, she said, "You go ahead," and I didn't hesitate. I took off my bathing suit, handed it to her, and splooshed right in.

Afterward, she rubbed some clay off my back and smeared it under her eyes. "You have my breasts," she said, as though I'd accomplished something.

I asked her to tell me about Archie Knox.

She glanced over at me, as though she still wasn't sure I was worth telling things to. Then she said, "He used to be very wild. In his martini days."

"Wild how?" I asked.

"Women," she said. "Women just loved him." She told me there was a story about one very young woman who'd committed suicide. I waited for her to go on, but she didn't. She was quiet. Then she brightened. "And dogs," she said.

"Dogs?" I asked.

"Dogs followed him everywhere."

— • —

"He was some sort of boxing champion," she told me the night she took me out to celebrate my graduation. "He was always punching someone in the nose."

"Macho," I said.

"No," she said. "It was the clarity of expression that appealed to him."

— • —

I was twenty-five before I saw Archie Knox again. It was at a party on Central Park West, which I attended as the guest of a guest of a guest. I was an editorial assistant at H—— by then and the youngest person at the party.

I nodded to him across the room, and as he came toward me, I saw that his hair had turned white.

"What're you drinking?" he asked me.

"Scotch and soda," I said.

A moment later, he returned and handed me a glass of milk. "Somebody has to take care of you," he said, and disappeared.

My friend from H—— left. I stood by myself, trying to appear captivated, until only a few people remained.

Archie came up to me. He took my elbow and said, "Let's get you something to eat."

I assumed he knew who I was, but when I mentioned my aunt, he said, "I'll be damned."

Over supper, I asked him about K———, where he was the editorial director. He didn't want to talk about that.

He told me my aunt was the most beautiful woman alive, even at eighty. He touched my chin, and moved my head from side to side, studying my profiles. He smiled and said, "No resemblance at all."

———•———

I met Archie at a French restaurant for supper before the theater. After the waiter had taken our order, I mentioned that my boyfriend, Jamie, was probably in Paris right now. Jamie had been in Europe for a month, trying to figure out what to do with his life—which was what he was doing with his life.

"Who is this Jamie person?" Archie asked.

"I told you," I said, and picked a crayon out of the glass and began doodling on the paper tablecloth.

"Does he make you happy?"

"Sure," I said.

He told me I didn't know what real happiness was. "You have to shrink yourself to fit into this little life with him."

I put my crayon down. "You don't know what you're talking about."

He told me I was made for something bigger. He said, "You're old enough to know better."

I said, "Don't you think you're a little old for me?"

"No," he said. Our drinks came and he downed his club soda in one long gulp, his Adam's apple rising and falling. He put money and the theater tickets on the table and stood. He said, "I think you're too young for me." Then he walked out.

———•———

He didn't apologize, or even mention it, when he called to invite me over for dinner.

He lived in a brownstone in the West Village, two whole floors to himself. I asked for a tour. Every room reminded me of a study—dark, heavy wood and leather, a little shabby, books and manuscripts everywhere.

Only his study was uncluttered. It was plain, just an ancient typewriter on a mahogany desk.

I followed him down the hall. "Guest room," he said, and I peered in. There was a breakfront full of boxing trophies—silver and gold statuettes with their little dukes up.

Two doors down, he said, "I assume you'd prefer to skip the master bedroom."

"Correct," I said.

He said, "Excuse me," opened the door and pretended to speak to someone inside. "I'll be up soon, darling," he said. He paused as though listening to a response. "Don't be silly," he said. "I'm just feeding a hungry child."

In the kitchen, he cut up a lime and apologized for not having wine to offer me.

I was noticing all the doodads on his windowsill—a ceramic rhino, a marble egg, a souvenir glass ball of snowy

Nebraska. They were like the presents I'd given Jamie, and I was wondering who'd given Archie his, when he said, "I don't keep any alcohol in the house."

He handed me a glass of seltzer. "I haven't had a drink for two years," he said.

I almost said, *You must be pretty thirsty,* when I saw how he was looking at me, and he looked at me like that for a long time to let me know the importance of his words.

———•———

At Caffè Vivaldi, Archie asked me if I knew Dante's definition of hell.

I sipped my cappuccino. "Give me a minute," I said.

"Proximity without intimacy," he said.

"Listen, Dante." I was going to remind him about Jamie, but instead I said, "I just don't feel that way about you."

He said, "Spare me the juvenalia."

———•———

Archie and I were having dinner at a restaurant in Midtown when the publicist of H—— came over to our table. "Hello all," she said.

Afterward, I said, "Now everyone's going to think we're having an affair."

"Well," Archie said, "we fooled them."

———•———

For my birthday, Archie gave me his novel, his first, he said, and only. It was almost as old as I was. The book was about a boy growing up with his mother in

Nebraska, and I read it straight through, sitting on the futon on the floor of my tiny apartment. When I finished, I called my best friend, Sophie.

She said, "I wouldn't care if he was Hemingway."

"You mean because he's an alcoholic. Because he's twice my age."

She reminded me that he was more than twice my age. "But no," she said. "I mean because he's larger than life."

——•——

Jamie left a message on my answering machine, telling me how much he missed me and that he was delaying his return another week or so.

I called Archie. "You want to go to the movies?"

"No," he said. "All right."

The only movie he wanted to see was *Key Largo* at the revival house on Eighth Street. Afterward, walking out, he told me that while Bogart was dying, Lauren Bacall slept with Frank Sinatra. "Don't ever do that to me, okay, honey?"

I said, "I don't even like Frank Sinatra."

So, back at his house, he put on a Sinatra record. "Don't tell me you don't think that's beautiful," he said.

I said, "You're scaring me."

——•——

In a cab home from a jazz club, he said, "You act like I just want to sleep with you."

He said, "I want to everything with you."

Which was when I touched him for the first time.

I slid my fingers underneath his sleeve and touched his forearm.

He took my other hand. "But if you just want to sleep with me, that's okay, too."

The cab pulled up in front of my building. "Call me if you change your mind," he said.

I nodded and got out.

He leaned out the cab window. "Call me any time of the night or day."

Upstairs, Jamie was asleep in my bed.

———•———

I had forgotten everything nice about Jamie, and especially the main thing. His fingertips swirled as light as smoke on my skin, and my body gave in right away, before I told myself, *You can't be blamed for what you do in your sleep.*

We had breakfast in the diner around the corner.

"So," Jamie said, "what've you been doing?"

"Nothing," I said, and coughed. "Thinking a lot."

He nodded, putting some jelly on his toast.

I said, "I've been thinking we shouldn't go on like this."

"Like what?" he said. "I've been away for two months."

I said, "I feel like I have to shrink myself to fit into our life together."

"Well, cut that shit out," he said, and grinned. "I missed you."

"Look," I said. "I think there's somebody else."

"Jesus," he said, and his voice got a little mean with exasperation. "There is nobody else."

"There is," I said.

That made him sit up. It was the first time he'd sat up in a long while, if he ever had, and I admit I was glad to see it.

———•———

I called Archie, but the phone rang and rang. I picked up his novel and read it again. I was still holding it when I woke up.

In the morning, I took a walk over there. I knocked on his door, waited and knocked again.

The door opened. "Well," Archie said.

His hair was sticking out funny, and even though he was smiling, he didn't seem glad to see me.

I wondered if he already had a guest over.

"Come in," he said.

The house seemed big and dark and formal. We sat down at the big mahogany table in the dining room.

I told him about finding Jamie in my apartment and breaking up with him the next morning.

He said, "About time," and came over to me. I stood, I held him, and we kissed, but it was not what I expected it to be.

———•———

He lit cigarettes for both of us and lay back. He was quiet, so I was; he was thinking, so I did.

We lay there in the dark.

I said, "What?"

He didn't answer for a long time, so long I thought he wouldn't. Then, finally, he said, "Everything."

Even now, remembering the sound of his voice chastens every word I say.

———•———

In the evenings, he'd work upstairs in his study, and I'd edit manuscripts at the big mahogany table, where I could worry a sentence for an hour.

He'd come down to refill his iced tea and look in on me. "What is it?" he'd ask.

Standing behind me, he'd read. He'd take the pencil out of my hand and cross out a word or a sentence or the whole page. "There," he'd say. It took him about thirty seconds, and he was always right.

———•———

Each time, Archie was mystified. Each time, he told me it had only happened to him once, years ago, when he was blind drunk. He'd light our cigarettes and lie there, staring straight ahead.

"It's not you, babe," he said one night.

I nodded, as though consoled. The thought had never occurred to me.

———•———

He took me to a literati dinner party and introduced me as "The Rising Star of H———."

I was shy, so I talked too much.

The men smiled indulgently.

The women were unfailingly gracious.

When we were undressing for bed, I said, "They think I'm a bimbo."

"Bimbo sounds masculine," he said. "Bimba."

"This bothers me," I said.

"Honey," he said, "they're just jealous."

"Just jealous."

"Right," he said. "We're the only happy couple I know."

———•———

He couldn't believe all the great old movies I'd missed. "Your whole generation is culturally bankrupt," he said. He set about trying to educate me.

After watching the original *Thin Man*, he said, "You're like Nora, and I'm like Nick. We're like Bogart and Bacall. Like Hepburn and Tracy."

I said, "More like Mr. Wilson and Dennis the Menace."

———•———

We had Sophie over for dinner.

Archie told her about pursuing me, the party on Central Park West, the publicist, and the Sunday I knocked on his door. "Finally," he said, "Jane gives in. We go upstairs. I take off my clothes. I take off hers—"

"You want coffee?" I asked.

"No, thanks," Sophie said.

Archie glared at me. "She's a little nervous, she says, 'Can we talk?' 'Sure,' I say. 'No prob.' I get cigarettes. We lie there, smoking and talking. Of course, I can't concentrate—"

"Dessert?"

Sophie said, "Not for me."

"So," Archie went on, "I'm waiting for her to finish her cigarette." He made his voice low. "I'm about to give up when she gives me this little nod, and she sits up to put out her cigarette." He paused. "And she drops a live ash on my chest!"

I stared at him: *What are you talking about? That was a whole other night.*

He was watching Sophie laugh.

He said, "She starts a brushfire in my chest hair! The gazelles leap out and then the elephants stampede . . ."

Sophie was still laughing when she looked over at me, and her expression said, *Okay, now I get it.*

———•———

I stored up jokes and anecdotes to tell him. I practiced them in my head.

"How was the dentist?" he asked.

"You know what he told me?" I said. "I should be brushing my gums! Did you ever hear of that?" I paused. "My hairdresser will probably tell me I should be brushing my neck!"

He laughed, almost against his will. "You're so weird," he said.

———•———

At a publication party, I overheard him say, ". . . so Jane accuses me of being an anti-Semite."

I was behind him, at the bar, and I took my wine from the bartender and stayed where I was.

Archie said, "I remind her that my ex-wife is Jewish, and Jane says, 'What does that prove? Every misogynist I know is married.' "

The man he was talking to said, "Very clever."

In the cab, I said, "What was that anti-Semite thing about? And the other night with Sophie. You know, I don't want to just be some made-up character in your anecdotes."

"*To be just,*" he said.

"What does justice have to do with anything?" I said.

He said, "Good editors don't split infinitives."

"You're correcting my grammar now?"

"Yes," he said. "I'm helping you to be better. And I expect the same from you."

I said, "What if I don't want to be better?"

He said, "Then you'll be just a petulant, infinitive-splitting eavesdropper."

—•—

I gave up my apartment and moved in.

—•—

I had to tell my family then.

My parents were very quiet.

My brother said, "Can't you find kids your own age to play with?"

My aunt was very old by then, and I hadn't seen her for a long time. After I told her about Archie, she closed her eyes, and I thought maybe she'd fallen asleep. Finally, she said, "A young woman does a lot for an older man."

I said, "It's not like that." I wanted to convince her. I said, "We think alike."

"Oh, my dear," she said. "A man thinks with his dick."

———•———

The doctor assured Archie everything would be fine as soon as they got his blood sugar under control. It was good news. He came home with a gadget, The Pricker, we called it.

He'd never liked me to see him inject his insulin, but with The Pricker he was different. It was our project. He'd press the button and the pin would nip out and prick his finger. I'd take his finger and smear the blood on the treated paper and put it into the gizmo. While we waited for the reading, I'd guess how sweet his blood was.

———•———

At home, he read a novel, lying on the leather sofa in the den, an iced tea and a bowl of colossal olives on the end table. He turned on PBS. He called out, "*American Masters* is on —it's Irving Berlin."

I didn't move.

He refilled his iced tea, and said, "What's the matter with you?"

"Nothing."

I listened to the sound of his slippers shuffling back to the living room.

In bed, he said, "I don't know who you are, but I want Jane back." He started kissing me. "What have you done with my Jane?"

I laughed.

"Ah, well," he said. "Any port in a storm."

———•———

He called in his blood-sugar results, and the doctor adjusted his insulin dosage. We waited for the big change. He was still supposed to monitor his blood sugar. I don't know when he stopped. I found The Pricker way in the back of the pantry, behind his supply of syringes.

———•———

We spent weekends at his farmhouse in the Berkshires. The first time I saw his car, a white Lincoln Continental, I couldn't believe it. I said, "It was nice of your father to lend you his car."

"It's very comfortable," he said, making his voice creaky and old.

It was like riding in a living room.

———•———

His farmhouse was a century old, and the walls slanted and sloped, the kitchen had a checkerboard floor, every window looked out on a meadow. We took our meals outside. In the evenings, we visited his friends or played Billie Holiday on the ancient record player and danced.

———•———

He went to a specialist at Mass. General, and was told he couldn't expect his body to work right as long as he kept smoking.

We quit.

We drank fruit juice. We did breathing exercises. When he wanted a cigarette, he took a nap. I wept.

He felt better, he said. No more spots in front of his eyes. His feet didn't tingle. But those were the only changes.

—•—

"I wouldn't blame you if you left me," he said.

"No," I said.

"If the roles were reversed," he said, "I'd leave you."

—•—

Driving up to the farmhouse he spoke about the first girl he slept with. He said, "When I was coming, I had to keep myself from saying, 'Marry me, marry me, marry me.' "

Over breakfast, he told me that his ex-wife, Frances Gould, was the smartest woman he'd ever known. He met her at graduate school at Yale. She had custody of their daughter, Elizabeth, and he called them on Sundays.

He referred to Frances as "Elizabeth's mother"—as in "I'm afraid Elizabeth's mother is still in love with me."

—•—

At the grocery store, a woman with big cheekbones came up to us, and I recognized her as the beauty from the first time I saw Archie.

"Corky," he said, and they kissed. "This is Jane."

They talked about their daughters. Corky's was having a tough time with the girls at school, but the boys adored her. Corky said, "I've never understood women."

—•—

While we unpacked the groceries, Archie told me that Corky had been his mistress on and off for a dozen years.

She was a big party girl, he said, she'd bring anybody home, but she drew a blank in the bedroom. "It was the saddest thing," he said.

"Sad," I said.

He glanced over at me. "She was abused as a child."

"Oh," I said.

I watched him thinking about Corky.

He said, "She was once the most magnificent woman on earth to look at."

"So," I said, "what makes you think I want to hear about this?"

"What?"

"All these women," I said.

He said, "It's my life I'm telling you about."

I said, "What's your point?"

He told me that he'd lived for fifty-four years before knowing me, and those fifty-four years made him the man he was. The man I loved. I shouldn't begrudge him those experiences, and there was no reason for me to be jealous of any woman.

I told him I thought I understood.

"Good," he said.

I said, "Let me tell you about the men I've known."

—·—

The night we went to my aunt's for dinner it was raining out, and I wondered if weather still affected her. She seemed to me now both meaner and kinder than she'd ever been.

She answered the door herself, and she looked wiry, in a loose, white turtleneck.

Archie kissed her forehead.

She was wearing lipstick, but the contour was off. I said, "Excuse us," and took her elbow.

In the bathroom, when I uncapped the lipstick, she said, "I can do it." She looked at me in the mirror. "You could use a little color yourself."

I told her I didn't wear makeup.

She said, "That's a mistake."

Once we were seated in the living room, the nurse brought three glasses of champagne on a tray, and I stared as Archie took his. He avoided my eyes, and held on to the stem of the glass. He lifted the champagne. He swirled it.

"Jane won't let me drink," he said to my aunt.

She said her nurse was just as bad.

During dinner, my aunt said, "Jane used to ask me to tell her stories about you."

When he said, "What did you tell her?" I felt sick, though I could not have said why.

She said, "I didn't tell her what a mean drunk you can be."

——•——

The night I found out she died, Archie and I lay on the sofa for a long time in the dark. He combed my hair with his fingers. When he got to a knot, he'd give it a little yank.

I wanted to feel worse than I felt, so I tried to think of the best time I had with my aunt, but I couldn't remember anything. I was going to ask Archie for his memory of her, but when I turned around, his face looked strange in the dark. "What?" I said.

He said, "Your family will be coming in."

———•———

Archie asked me to invite them over for brunch, but I told him they probably wouldn't have time before the service, and that's what my mom told me. "We'll try," she said.

Archie bought lox and bagels anyway, and set the table with lilies. All morning, he kept looking at his watch, as though he'd been stood up.

When we heard the knocker, Archie rose, but he let me go to the door.

It was just my brother. Henry kissed my cheek and said, "Dad said just to meet at the place."

I saw my dad and mom in the car, and walked out the door with Henry, who nudged me and said, "Cushy digs."

I stuck my head in the car window and kissed my father. "Hi, Papa," I said, and he said, "Hi, love."

"I'm sorry we're so late," my mom said, leaning forward to let Henry in the backseat.

I wanted to go with them.

Maybe my father could tell. He said, "We'll meet you there."

"Okay," I said.

I watched the car drive around the corner, and I turned to go inside. Archie was standing at the door, looking out.

———•———

A lot of people came to the funeral and almost as many to the cemetery. Most of them were old, and Archie seemed to know all of them.

There was no chance to talk until after the burial. We all stood around the Lincoln. It started to rain, and I could tell my father wanted to get going back to Philadelphia, but the people Archie knew kept interrupting to talk to him.

Finally, my father said, "We've got to get back."

Archie said, "We were hoping you'd stay for dinner."

Henry mouthed to me, *Nice car.*

"Next time," my mom said, and Archie kissed her cheek.

A guy in a black slicker was directing cars, and Archie got in his. I kissed everyone, but I didn't want to leave.

The guy motioned to the Lincoln, and Archie leaned over to the passenger side and knocked on the window. His voice was muted when he said, "Come on, honey."

"Hey," the guy in the slicker called to me, "tell your dad to pull out."

My parents pretended they hadn't heard. Henry looked over at me. He smiled.

———•———

On the way back from the cemetery, I kept seeing Archie as the old man my brother saw. So I looked out the window.

Archie knew it had gone badly, but you could tell he was trying to reassure himself that he'd done everything he could.

When we got to the West Side Highway, the lanes narrowed. On the back of a truck, there was a flashing arrow, but the arrow part was out. "It's like a hyphen," I said.

Archie smiled at me. "Danger," he said. "Compound words ahead."

———•———

That night he told me about the girlfriend of his who'd committed suicide. I knew he was telling me the truth, and that it was the worst thing that had ever happened to him. It was unlike any other story he'd ever told me. He didn't improve details, or pace it for suspense. When he finished, he said, "Please don't ever tell that to anyone."

"No," I said. "I won't."

———•———

I heard him talking on the phone in his study, and his voice was low and intimate. After he hung up, he found me in the kitchen. "Elizabeth's mother is in town," he said. "She wants to meet you."

"Goody," I said.

He ignored me. "You know what she said when I told her I plan to marry you? 'Well, old dear, I guess love is the real suspension of disbelief.'"

I said, "I heard how you talked to her."

"Jesus," he said. He told me he hadn't so much as looked at another woman since he'd met me. Then his voice changed. "Which is more than you can say."

I said, "What're you talking about?"

"The night you found Jamie in your apartment," he said. "Your final fuck."

I stood there.

"I thought so," he said.

———•———

He wouldn't speak to me. He slept in the guest room, and he was gone when I woke up.

At work, I was a zombie.

I called Sophie. "Cut the guy a break," she said, and reminded me that I got jealous of women he hadn't seen in thirty years.

"It's different," I said. "I think of the sex he used to have."

She said, "It's the same for him."

———•———

I brought home shrimp and bread and an armful of flowers. The hall was dark. "Honey?" I called.

I thought, *He's up there with Elizabeth's mother.*

Still carrying the shrimp and flowers, I went upstairs. The bedroom door was closed, and I opened it, slowly. The room was dark. It was empty.

I saw the light coming from the study. I smelled cigarette smoke.

He was sitting at his desk, wearing a T-shirt and boxers, socks and slippers. He didn't turn around.

"Honey?" I said, and then I saw the martini.

I couldn't breathe right.

I stared at the glass until everything else blurred out. It was just the glass and me. The glass was large and elegant, shapely.

A voice said, *Nobody drinks from a glass like that at home.*

Maybe he just brought it out to look at.

He could just be reminiscing.

He might just be flirting.

You don't know.

He swiveled around in his desk chair, and I saw his eyes. He squinted at me, and it was his voice, but it wasn't him when he said, "What're *you* looking at?"

———•———

After a week, I packed my stuff.

I went up to his study.

He didn't turn around. "You're the one who did something wrong," he said. "And you're punishing me for it."

"Look," I said, and my voice was thin and false. "The reason I'm leaving is because of the booze."

"Jesus," he said. *"The reason is because?"*

I realized I was waiting for his permission to leave.

———•———

He called me sometimes, late. I'd listen for the alcohol in his voice. I couldn't always hear it right away, but it was always there. After a while, I didn't answer the phone anymore. I let my machine pick up.

Once, in the middle of the night, I did answer. He

told me he was killing himself, and I took a cab over there.

The door was unlocked and all the lights were on. He was up in his study.

"Well, hello," he said. He smiled.

I told him he didn't seem like he was about to kill himself.

"I was being figurative." He said, "Listen to this," and he picked up a page from a manuscript, and read.

It took me a minute to understand that he was reading his own prose. It was a novel, and it opened with that party on Central Park West.

When he'd finished reading, he said, "See?"

"No," I said.

"The guy you say I am couldn't have written that page."

"I never said anything,"

He said, "People wait their whole lives for the kind of happiness we have."

———•———

The publisher called me into his office. He told me that he'd just received a novel by Archie Knox, an exclusive submission. "I've never liked Archie," he said. "And Archie has never liked me."

I nodded and stopped myself.

"He'll sell it to us on the condition that you edit it."

I didn't move.

"Take a look at it," he said. "It's a fast read."

He held out the manuscript.

"You wouldn't have to change a word," he said.

"No," I said.

He looked at me for the first time. "I completely understand," he said.

———•———

I read the book as soon as it came out from S———. Everyone did. It was published in the summer, and I would walk on the beach and see people reading it.

I still look for the paperback in stores. I open it up to the dedication page to see my name. Sometimes I turn to the first page, and I remember the night he read it to me, and how he leaned back in his chair and said, "See?"

The writing is clean. I really wouldn't have changed a word. Most of it is true, too, except that the hero quits drinking and the girl grows up. On the last page, the couple gets married, which is a nice way for a love story to end.

THE
BEST POSSIBLE
LIGHT

Since having children does mean giving up so much, good parents naturally do, and should, expect something from their children in return: not spoken thanks for being born or being cared for . . . but . . . willingness to accept the parents' standards and ideals.

—From *The Common Sense Book of Baby and Child Care* by Benjamin Spock, M.D.

Out of nowhere, my son, Barney, shows up. I'm in the kitchen, making mint iced tea and singing along with opera, when I hear the downstairs buzzer. Through the intercom, Barney calls out, imitating himself at eight, "Open up! Mom! It's me!" I buzz him in and go to the landing. He's already rounding the second floor, and in the dim light I see his jeans and T-shirt. As ever, he has brought a woman with him.

Barney is thirty-four but looks twenty-one. He's short and muscular, dark-skinned, and he has a great nose. I see his face for only a second before he's hugging me. I'm saying, "What are you doing here? I can't believe you're here."

He takes his girlfriend's arm and, in a put-on British accent, he says, "Meet me sainted mum."

"Call me Nina," I say.

"How do you do?" she says, and shakes my hand. "I'm

Laurel." She's taller than he is, and handsome. She wears her dark blonde hair in a braid.

Barney lives in Chicago and I'm waiting for him to tell me what he's doing here in New York, and why the surprise, but Laurel just says, "I hope we're not intruding."

Barney says, "Don't be silly."

I swat him.

I lead them out to my terrace, brush the leaves off the seats and table, and get the mint tea. From the kitchen, I call out, "You hungry?" and Barney answers no for both of them. Which is lucky, since all I have in the refrigerator is celery and yogurt.

Out on the terrace, Barney and Laurel sit close together; he has his arm around her, his fingers on her neck.

Laurel sits up straight in her chair, like a dancer. She puts two heaping teaspoons of sugar in her tea, smiles apologetically, and pours in another.

"How long can you stay?" I ask.

Barney says they're going to Laurel's parents' in Woods Hole tomorrow. "They're marine biologists," he says. "A family of scientists."

Now I remember Barney talking about a woman who worked in a lab. I don't listen as closely as I used to; since his divorce, he always has a girlfriend—he gets all wrapped up, but a few months later when I ask how it's going, he sounds vague and irritable.

I say, "You're a scientist, Laurel?"

She nods.

"I told you," he says. "She's an entomologist."

She says, "I study bugs." She looks around her, and at the trees, which are still in bloom. The sunlight passes through the branches and makes speckles of warm light on the brick floor. "It's so pretty out here," she says. "I didn't know there were apartments like this in New York."

I explain that Greenwich Village isn't like the rest of the city. "It's small New York," I say.

When she asks about the for sale sign on the building, I tell her the saga of the owner trying to buy me and my upstairs neighbor out of our leases.

"How is the beautiful Miss Rita?" Barney asks.

"She died about two years ago," I say. "She was almost ninety, I think."

"She was a babe," he tells Laurel.

"She was a writer," I say, looking at my son.

He says, "So who's upstairs?"

"Her niece, Jane."

Barney says, "Does she look like Rita?"

"Anyway," I say to Laurel, "I'm here forever."

"That's lucky," she says.

"I could never live here again," Barney says. He sings, "Got those New York real estate blues."

I ask Barney if he's been at Kingston Mines, the blues club where he's been playing sax on and off for years.

He says, "I've been doing other stuff," and I can tell he doesn't want to talk about it. He leans back and picks the dead leaves off of my geranium. "So, Nina," he says. "What about a dinner party?"

"What *about* a dinner party?"

"Great idea." He says, "I'll round up the usual suspects," meaning his sisters. He gets the phone from the kitchen and brings it outside to us. He calls the restaurant and says, "Isabelle, please. Tell her it's Jerry Kinkaid." The name is familiar, and I suddenly remember Isabelle's greaser boyfriend from seventh grade. Barney makes his voice raspy and says, "Babe. Meet me at the tracks." He holds the phone out so we can hear Isabelle laughing. He clowns around with her, but he means to entertain us, too. He sings, "I'll Build a Stairway to Paradise," and hams it up; he dances, marching with a branch for a walking stick. Barney is always making everyone fall in love with him.

After he hangs up, he calls P. K. at the office. She's the youngest, a civil-rights lawyer. With her, Barney turns serious. "Hey, Peanut," he says. He smiles at Laurel, and takes the phone inside.

So I'm out on the terrace alone with Laurel. We're both quiet, and then she asks me about the documentary I produced about doormen. Barney showed it to her, and she tells me which doormen she liked best. She looks right at me while I talk, and I can tell she is really listening.

Barney comes back out and stands behind Laurel's chair. "We've got P. K., Isabelle and her beau—what's his name?"

I'm not sure. "Giancarlo?"

"That's it," he says.

"P. K. isn't bringing Roger?"

"Archived," he says. Very lightly he touches Laurel's neck and jaw and cheeks. "You need a nap, Bugsy?" He kisses the top of her head, and it occurs to me that I have not seen him this gentle with anyone since Julie, his ex-wife.

I tell Barney they'll stay in my room. I straighten it up, get towels, and Laurel helps me make up the bed with fresh sheets. Barney says to me, "I'm just going to sing her to sleep."

I go back to the terrace and sit down with my shopping list for the party. When Barney comes out, he doesn't sit with me, he hoists himself up on the wall.

I'd like to ask about Julie. I start to and stop. It feels strange with Laurel lying down in my room. But Julie was a part of this family; you don't just forget. Finally, I say, "Have you seen Julie at all?"

"I have." He smiles, and it's insolent or sexual or mischievous, a bad-boy smile.

"How is she?"

"Great."

I give him a look.

He says, "Laurel and I had dinner with her Thursday."

Now he's serious, thinking about something. He says, "How's Dad?"

Barney never asks about his father. I say, "Dad?"

"Sure."

I tell him that his father's in a new gallery, a good one.

I ask him if he wants to see the invitation to the opening, and Barney says, again, "Sure."

I get Ben's card from the mail tray. It's a beautiful invitation—three tiny reproductions of his paintings. I hand the card to Barney and say, "It's next Friday."

Barney glances at the invitation and says, "Now there's a must-miss."

He sits opposite me while I finish my shopping list.

"I can get this stuff," he says.

I say, "What have you done with my son?"

He smiles. "I don't know what you mean."

——•——

P. K. is the first to arrive. She comes straight from work, so she's got on a suit and is carrying a big briefcase. P. K. is a little plump, but on her it's pretty, childlike, and soft. Her face is flushed from climbing the stairs, and her eyes are expectant. She kisses me and whispers, "Is Julie here?"

I say no and she sighs. "It was the way he said 'we.' I don't know." She thinks a minute. "It's dumb."

"He's brought Laurel," I say. "She's very nice."

"Great," she says with zero enthusiasm. "Where is he?"

"Liquor store."

Laurel comes out of the bedroom. She's just gotten up. "Hi," she says.

A few minutes later, P. K. follows me into the kitchen; she's taken off her stockings and shoes and put on my black T-shirt over her pleated skirt. "This one is no bimbo," she says softly.

I put her to work on the salad.

Laurel joins us. Now she's awake, and her hair is loose and curly to her shoulders. "How can I help?" she asks, and P. K. hands her the lettuce.

Barney comes back from the liquor store. When he sees P. K. he puts the bags down right where he is, which happens to be on the living-room floor, and hugs her. "Well, Counselor," he says, rubbing her back.

He sets up the dining room, and turns on the radio. Gladys Knight's version of "Heard It Through the Grapevine" is on. We're all dancing and singing, "Guess you wonder how I knew," when Isabelle and Giancarlo arrive.

Isabelle is the great beauty of the family. Tonight she's wearing motorcycle boots that make her look like she's nine feet tall. "Hey, you," she says, hugging Barney. She introduces Giancarlo all around. He's got a square jaw and long dark hair, and he is very handsome, very Italian.

When Barney introduces Laurel, Isabelle is breezy. She plays the glamour-puss, but that's not who she really is.

There's no room for her and Giancarlo in the kitchen, so they take drinks to the living room. I tell P. K. to go keep them company, but she says, "You go, Barney."

We all settle into the living room for cocktails. I'm on the footstool, and Barney leans all the way down to me and says in my ear, "They're bonding," meaning P. K. and Laurel. He kisses my head and stands up.

"Hey you guys," Isabelle says. "I've got a surprise." She turns to Laurel. "Has Barney told you anything about Water Mill?"

"A little."

"That's where Barney and I spent our formative years. It was a cooperative farm." To Giancarlo, she says, "Comunista." She describes the apple orchards, the other families, and how we used to cross the river to hear folk concerts.

P. K. is riveted. She feels she missed out on the good ol' days, and she isn't wrong.

Giancarlo is gazing at Isabelle, studying her face; I can't tell if he's madly in love or doesn't understand English.

"Cut to the chase, Iz," Barney says.

"No," P. K. says. "Go on."

Isabelle looks away from me, to Barney and then to P. K. and says, "Dad and I went up there last weekend." She pauses. "Remember we heard it was leveled?"

Barney nods.

"It was," she says. "Except for one thing." She takes photographs out of her bag. *"Voila!"* She passes them out.

They are pictures of the tiny village Barney built behind our house. We had the gardener's cottage, and Barney took over the huge flower bed at the end of the lawn. There was construction going on all over the estate, and Barney endeared himself to anyone who'd give him anything for his village. He got slate for the roofs, metal for his bridges, and blue glass for the swimming pools. He made hills and valleys, even a river, and dozens of brick-size houses out of his "secret formula"—a cement-and-stone mixture.

Now he gives Laurel a tour, pointing at the photograph. "Baseball diamond, drive-in movie theater . . ."

P. K. says, "It looks so real."

Isabelle says, "Because everything's gone. There's no scale."

Which stops me. I look at the picture. The place where our house once stood is smooth orange dirt, crisscrossed with bulldozer tracks. "It's a ghost town," I say.

Barney nods. "Yup," he says.

Isabelle says, "Your Topia."

Barney's expression is dreamy, and I can tell he is remembering.

Isabelle says to Laurel, "Barney overheard the grownups talking about Utopia."

I remember Ben's speeches about creating our own world, and for a second I am myself at thirty-four, sitting Indian-style, Barney's head in my lap; we're in a big circle with all the families, at the clearing in the apple orchard. It's a spring evening, and I can smell the blossoms. "We should question everything," Ben says. "Money, religion. Monogamy." I look over at my husband: *You don't mean us, do you, sweetheart?*

Now Laurel asks Barney, "How old were you?"

He looks at me. "Eight?"

"That's about right," I say.

"How long did it take you?" P. K. asks.

"The whole summer," Isabelle says.

P. K. says, "I love that they left it standing."

I go to the kitchen to check on dinner, and I overhear Barney say, "You see Dad a lot, Isabelle?"

We sit down to dinner. I've overcooked the pasta, but no one seems to notice. We're all talking and laughing, drinking wine, and I get this good feeling. We're all here.

Giancarlo, on my right, says, "Why did you leave the farm?" His English is perfect.

I tell him that the schools weren't great, and we were losing money on the apples. "It wasn't realistic."

Isabelle says, "Plus, it turned into a big orgy."

"Isabelle," I say.

"That's what Dad said."

"So," Laurel says, "you moved to Rome."

I tell her we meant to stay only a year but I found good work, and she says, "Doing what?"

"Dubbing," I say. "My voice is immortalized on dozens of spaghetti Westerns. Barney's, too."

"Pa!" Barney shouts. "Injuns!"

"How do you do it?" Laurel asks.

"You're adapting," I say. "You fit words into an actor's mouth."

Barney says, "It's hard, because Italian words usually end in vowels—openmouthed." He smiles at Giancarlo.

I say, "If the actor says, 'Prego,' you can't dub, 'You're welcome.' "

Barney and I act it out: I mouth "Prego" at the same time Barney says, "You're welcome."

Barney becomes instructor-like: "Regard the subtle differences between *u* and *i*." He leads us all through the consonants and vowels, and we watch one another's mouths. We are a tableful of sounds.

P. K. says, "I feel like I'm in first grade."

At dessert, I bring out champagne. P. K. makes the first toast: "To our honored guests from the Windy City!" and everyone clinks glasses.

Giancarlo stands up and says, "To our masterful chef!"

I tell Isabelle, "I like this one."

P. K. is describing her last case and why she didn't put the alleged drug dealer on the stand. "He was innocent," she says, "but he lied about everything." She's all animated, and I'm a little annoyed when Barney stands up and taps his spoon against his glass.

"I have something to announce," he says. "A major announcement." He smiles all around, and then pulls Laurel to her feet. "We're pregnant," he says.

They sit down. It takes a second for it to sink in, and then Isabelle jumps up and hugs them. "That's great," she says. "This is so great." Then we're all hugging one another and talking, a jangle of conversation.

Laurel half rises again, and says, "We're also getting married."

Everyone laughs; I have to admit, I'm relieved. The details circle the table—she saw the doctor last week, the wedding will be very soon, she's due in April.

"I'm going to be a grandmother," I say to myself.

Giancarlo squeezes my hand.

Then Barney stands again, still beaming.

Everyone thinks he's joking. "Sit down, you ham!"
P. K. calls out.

Isabelle says, "Give me a break!" She and Giancarlo
are laughing, and he kisses her.

Barney says, "There's something else."

I happen to look over at Laurel. She's pale and perspir-
ing; strands of her hair are sticking to her neck.

I say, "Sh."

Very slowly, Barney says, "Julie is pregnant, too."

Now we are all hushed.

Isabelle whispers to Giancarlo, "His ex-wife."

Barney's voice is steady. "I'm the father."

No one moves.

I watch my son. I don't think I've ever seen him look
so serious, but it doesn't seem real; it's as though he's imitating how someone responsible speaks. He says, "We're
going to help as much as we can." He seems to realize
that standing up isn't right—this isn't a toast—and he
abruptly sits down. "We're going to help," he says again.

P. K. is studying her brother. Out of all of us, she ex-
pects the most from him, and I can tell she wants to see
this whatever way he does. She will put it in the best possible light. For a second, her face clouds over with confu-
sion or disappointment, but then she looks at Barney,
straight and clear, and her voice is earnest when she says,
"Why are you doing this?"

Now Laurel speaks. She is a feat of self-possession. "We
decided together," she says. "It's the only thing to do."

We're all quiet again. Giancarlo leans forward and reaches his hand out to Barney. "Congratulations."

Isabelle says, "This is a soap opera."

Then, everyone turns to me, as though I'm going to deliver some kind of pronouncement. I get these voices in my head of what The Mother is supposed to say—maybe something about how it will all work out. My own mother would say something definite, final. I remember Ben and me telling my parents we were getting married. Their real objection was that he was Jewish, and a Communist, but my father bellowed, *The husband's role is to provide.* Now I look up at my own children.

"Barn," I say, "what about providing for children?"

He nods; he's got an answer ready. "I've been composing music for commercials."

Isabelle says, "Jingles," as though the frivolity of the word itself proves something.

Quietly, P. K. says, "Have you had any on TV?"

Barney nods, just barely. I think he's afraid she's going to ask him to hum one.

It is time for me to say, *Who wants coffee?* and when I do it's like dubbing.

Giancarlo nods, P. K. waves, Barney gives me a grateful look, but I shake my head and he knows to follow me into the kitchen.

I cannot bring myself to look at him. I hand him the kettle, he asks me which cups. I pour milk into a pitcher and say, "Do you have a date for the wedding?"

He says, "I think I should bring Laurel, don't you?"

I turn and face him.

For a long moment I see this man.

I see him and I think, *I am the one who taught him to regard himself as a blessing.*

"Jesus," he says, "I was just kidding." He backs away from me—almost into Isabelle.

She says, "May I have a word with you?"

They go out to the terrace, and before the door closes, we can all hear Isabelle say, "What the hell are you doing?"

Laurel comes in to help. She's industrious and quiet. Then she tells me how strange it was to meet Julie. She stops. "I didn't want to feel anything." She looks at me. She wants me to understand, and with my eyes I let her know that I do.

"I'm thirty-five," she says. "You try to plan your life, but that's not how it works." I can see how tired she is right now. "I love Barney," she says.

While we finish dessert, Isabelle's voice carries through the glass doors, but only an occasional word is clear— ". . . bullshit . . . responsibility . . . child . . ."

They walk inside. It's been raining, and Isabelle's white shirt is wet through in spots; it sticks to her skin. "Come on," she says to Giancarlo.

He shakes hands with Barney, whose hair has a wet sheen to it. Isabelle kisses everyone all around, and embraces Laurel. I see Laurel's shoulders rise and fall in a sigh. When Isabelle gets back to Barney, she says, "I'll be talking to you, bud."

"Yup," he says.

She gives him a quick hug. "Walk me to the door?" she says to me.

As soon as we're out on the landing, she says, "Don't tell me to go easy on him, Nina." She looks right at me, into my eyes. "He comes flying in here like Supersperm. And we're all supposed to congratulate him." Her voice softens. "It's not good for him."

Giancarlo stands with his hands in his jacket pockets. "Thank you for dinner," he says. He's on the top step when he turns around. "I think," he says, "you are a good family."

Isabelle is two steps below him, and she reaches out and holds on to his knees. "That's a very sentimental thing to say, you know." She laughs, and he grabs her. He picks her up and tries to carry her down the stairs. Over his shoulder, she waves to me.

Barney and Laurel are in the kitchen doing the dishes, and P. K. is rubbing Laurel's shoulders. "That feels great," Laurel says.

"We should go to bed," I say.

Barney yawns. "We're almost finished."

P. K. says good night to them, and she and I go into my bedroom. She takes off the T-shirt she borrowed from me and grabs her own blouse. She's standing in front of me in her bra, and I notice how white her skin is. She's hardly been in the sun at all this summer, she's been working so hard.

At the door, she says, "I don't think it's so bad."

I nod, not exactly in agreement. Her devotion to her brother, to all of us, takes my breath away.

THE

WORST THING A

SUBURBAN GIRL

COULD IMAGINE

Keep a calm atmosphere and children won't worry.

—From *The Sailor's Handbook,*
Edited by Halsey C. Herreshoff

My father knew he had leukemia for years before telling my brother and me. He explained that he hadn't wanted his illness to interfere with our lives. It had barely interfered with his own, he said, until recently. "I've been very lucky," he said, and I could tell he wanted us to see it this way, too.

This was an early spring weekend in the suburbs, and the three of us sat outside on the screened-in porch. My mother was in the background that afternoon, doing the brunch dishes and offering more coffee, weeding the garden and filling the bird feeder. It was warm but not hazy the way it can be in spring; the sky was blue with hefty clouds. The dark pink and red azaleas were just beginning to bloom.

—•—

Back in New York, I called my father before I left work. He was just getting home from the office. "Hi, love," he said. I knew he was in the kitchen, sipping a gin and tonic while my mother cooked dinner. His voice was as strong and reassuring as ever.

I tried to sound normal, too. Busy. When he asked what I was doing that night, I glanced at the newspaper open on my desk—a writer I'd heard on public radio was reading at a bookstore downtown—and I decided to go, so I could say so to my father.

After we hung up, I stared out of my window into the windows of the office building across the street. This was the year everyone started saying, "Work smart instead of long," and the offices were deserted, except for the tiny shapes of cleaning women in their grayish-blue uniforms, one or two on every floor. The woman would go into an office and clean. A second later the light would go out, and she would go on to the next office.

I heard the cleaning woman on my own floor, emptying wastebaskets and moving her custodial cart down the hall.

Her name was Blanca, and she was my social life.

———•———

I'd been a rising star at H—— until Mimi Howlett, the new executive editor, decided I was just the lights of an airplane.

The week she arrived she took me to lunch. At the restaurant, people turned around. Some knew Mimi and waved, but others just looked at her because she was beautiful enough for them to wonder if she was famous, and she carried herself as though she was.

I couldn't help staring, either—it was like she was a different species from me. She had the lollipop proportions of a model—big head, stick figure—pale skin, wintergreen eyes, and a nose barely big enough to breathe out of. That day, she was wearing a fedora, a charcoal-colored suit with a short jacket and an ankle-length skirt, and delicate laced-up boots. She might've been a romantic heroine from a novel, *The Age of Innocence* maybe, except she was with me, in my sacky wool dress, a worker in a documentary about the lumpen proletariat.

Her voice now: it was soft and whispery, the sound of perfume talking, which made her very occasional use of the word *fuck* as striking and even beautiful as a masculine man expressing nuanced and heartfelt emotion.

She began by telling me how sorry she was about my former boss, Dorrie, who'd been fired. She did seem sorry, and I hoped she was.

Then we talked about our favorite books— not recently published ones, but what we'd grown up reading and the classics we'd loved in college.

She'd gone to Princeton, she said, and asked where I'd gone. When I told her the name of my tiny college, she said that she thought she'd heard of it, adding, "I think the sister of a friend of mine went there."

She didn't mean to be disparaging, which only made me feel worse. Sitting across from her, I remembered all the rejections I'd gotten from colleges with median SAT scores hundreds of points lower than Princeton's. I remembered the thin envelopes, and how bad it felt to tell my father each night at dinner.

Mimi said, "Are you okay?"

"Yes," I said. "Do you mind if I smoke?"

—— • ——

I tried to avoid Mimi. Her presence seemed to call forth every rejection I'd ever experienced—the teachers who'd looked at me as though I held no promise, the boys who didn't like me back. Around her, I became fourteen again.

I doubt my reaction was new to her, but it couldn't have been pleasant. Even so, she tried to be kind and took me under her fluffy white wing.

She brought in lipsticks she no longer wore, silk scarves she thought I'd like. She let me know when a good sale was going on at Bergdorf or Barneys. She told me about an apartment, which my friend Sophie wound up taking.

The first time Mimi asked me to read one of her submissions, she said, "I thought you might be interested in this." But soon she was handing me stacks of manuscripts, every submission she didn't want to read herself, a terrible, endless supply. She did it in the nicest possible manner, as though asking a favor I was free to refuse.

Without realizing it, I became less the associate editor I'd been than an assistant she'd decided to bring up. She was forever interrupting herself to explain some basic aspect of publishing to me. I had to stop myself from saying, *Yes, I know,* which would've come across as an unwillingness to learn. And I did seem to know less and less.

After a while, she never seemed to look at me without assessing who I was and what I was capable of becoming. I could tell she doubted my devotion, and in this she was perfectly justified.

—•—

That afternoon, she'd held up her bottle of perfume, and I'd brought my wrists forward to be sprayed, as usual. Then she said that an agent had called asking about *Deep South*, a lyrical novel he'd submitted weeks ago —*Did I know anything about it?* I told her I'd look for it.

I knew where it was, of course—under my desk, where I hid all the manuscripts I hadn't read for her. Now I put *Deep South* in my book bag, said good night to Blanca, and headed downtown for the reading.

The bookstore was so crowded that I had to stand along the back shelves. Someone was already up at the microphone welcoming everyone. I was taking off my jacket and folding it over my book bag, when I heard the welcomer say, ". . . his editor, Archie Knox."

Since we'd broken up, I'd seen Archie a few times at readings and book parties. The first time, I went up to him, but he barely nodded before turning his back on me. My friend Sophie told me that he avoided me because he cared so much, but that wasn't how it felt.

From where I stood, he didn't look older or different. He wore an oatmeal Shetland-wool sweater I knew. He was saying that he'd read the book, *Loony*, straight through, forgetting dinner and postponing bed; he'd stayed up all night and eaten moo shu pork for breakfast, which he did not recommend. He paused and I saw him see me—his eyebrows pulled together—and he coughed and finished his story.

There was applause and then the author, Mickey Lamm, in a brown suit and sneakers, hugged Archie. Mickey looked exactly like his voice: bangs in his eyes and a bouncy walk; puppy-dog tails were what he was made of, though he was probably forty.

When the applause subsided, he said into the microphone, "Archie Knox, the best editor anywhere," and he clapped, and got the crowd clapping again with him. He had a crooked smile that didn't quite cover his teeth, and at about ninety words a minute he invited all the aspiring writers in the audience to send their manuscripts to Archie Knox at K——, and he gave the full address, including zip. In an announcer's voice he said, "That address again . . ." and repeated it.

I couldn't see where Archie was, but I could feel him there. I closed my eyes while Mickey read and pictured Archie holding a pencil above the manuscript.

Loony was a memoir of childhood, and the chapter Mickey read was about stealing pills from his psychiatrist stepfather's medicine cabinet. As it turned out, they were just anti-nauseants, though he and his friends imagined they'd discovered an excellent high—and he kept stealing those pills.

Mickey wasn't reading as much as being the boy

he'd been—daring devil, winking leprechaun, smiling sociopath—especially when he got caught stealing, and his stepfather asked, "Are you nauseated, Mickey?"

In the audience's laughter, I heard Archie's.

I couldn't bear the prospect of him ignoring me. After the applause, I got my stuff together fast. On my way out, I heard someone from the audience ask the standard question *What do you read for inspiration?* and Mickey's answer: "Bathroom walls."

———•———

I was living at my aunt Rita's old apartment in the Village. Legally, I wasn't supposed to be there so I hadn't really moved in. There wasn't room, anyway; no one had moved my aunt's stuff out. It seemed less defined by my presence than her absence, and the little terrace was the only place in it I liked to be.

But I couldn't read out there. So I got myself a tall diet root beer and a coaster, and took *Deep South* to her big formal dining-room table.

The novel started on flora (dark woods, tangled thickets, choking vines) and went to fauna—if bugs counted as fauna. Bugs, bugs, bugs—too small to see or as big as birds, swarms and loners, biting, stinging, and going up your nose. The prose was dense and poetic; it was like reading illegible handwriting, and after a few pages my eyes were just going left to right, word to word, not reading at all. So, when the phone rang, I answered on ring one.

Archie said, "It's me," though we'd been broken up for almost two years. "What's the matter?"

I was too surprised to answer. Then, I started crying and couldn't stop.

Archie hated to hear anyone cry—not because it hurt him or anything like that, he just hated crying. I could tell he was calling from a pay phone and knew that he was probably out to dinner with Mickey and his entourage, but he didn't say. He was silent, waiting for me to talk.

Finally, I got out: "My dad has leukemia."

All he said was, "Oh, honey," but in it I heard everything I needed to. He told me to blow my nose and come over to dinner the next night.

11

Archie answered the door, wearing the black cashmere sweater I'd given him as a Christmas present. "Hello, dear," he said. He sort of patted my shoulder.

Behind him I saw peonies on the dining-room table. They were white and edged with magenta, still closed into little fists. "Oh," I said. "My favorite."

He said, "Yes, I know," and his eyes said, *You're not yourself.*

While he poured club soda and squeezed lime into it, he told me that he'd stood over those peonies and asked, ordered, and begged them to open, but they were as resistant as I'd been at the beginning.

"Maybe they're seeing someone else," I said.

For dinner, we were having soft-shell crabs, another favorite of mine. While he sautéed them, I told him that my father didn't have the leukemia you usually heard about; it wasn't the kind that killed people right away.

"Good," Archie said.

I said, "But he's already had it for nine years."

Archie was setting our plates down on the dining-room table, and he stopped and turned around. "Nine years?"

I nodded.

We sat. I repeated what my father had said about not wanting the illness to interfere with my life, but I was afraid Archie would suspect what I did, so I said it out loud: "I think maybe he didn't think I could handle it or help him."

"No," Archie said, "he didn't want to put you through it." My father had been strong and noble, Archie said, which was how I was trying to see it, too.

I told him that my dad's doctor—Dr. Wischniak—had come over and explained the illness to Henry and me privately. I reminded Archie that I'd barely passed non-college-bound biology, but I understood that the leukemia and chemotherapy had weakened my father's immune system, and he'd become susceptible to infections, like the shingles and pneumonia he'd already had. I told Archie that my brother asked the doctor about the illness and the treatment; red cells and white ones, a bone-marrow transplant and blood transfusions. Then I asked my one question, *How much time does he have?* Dr. Wischniak said he couldn't answer that.

"No idea?" Archie said.

I shook my head.

I said that my question seemed to bother the doctor, and it sounded wrong to me, too, though I didn't understand why. "I felt like I'd spoken French in science class."

Archie said, "Maybe he just didn't like being asked a question he couldn't answer."

"Maybe," I said.

We took our coffee into the living room. He stood at the stereo and asked if I had any requests.

"*Something Blue*–ish," I said.

While he flipped through his records, he told me about the time he'd asked his daughter for requests; she was about three and cranky after a nap, going down the stairs one at a time on her butt. He imitated her saying, "No music, Daddy."

"I told her we had to listen to something," he said. "And she languorously put her hair on top of her head and like a world-weary nightclub singer said, 'Coltrane then.'"

That's what he put on now. I asked how Elizabeth was, and he said she was beautiful and smart and impressive, finishing her junior year at Stanford. She'd spent the year in Israel on a kibbutz. She'd forgiven him, he said, and they'd grown close; he might meet her in Greece over the summer.

I said that I'd been hoping to go to Greece that summer myself, but I wasn't sure now.

He sat beside me on the sofa, and patted my hand.

When we talked about Mickey's reading, I admitted that I hadn't read *Loony* yet, and Archie promised to get a copy to me. I could see how proud he was of the book, and I was wondering if I'd ever felt that way or would, when he asked what I'd acquired recently.

"Malaise," I said. I wasn't ready to pinpoint how nowhere my career was. "I have a new boss," I said.

"Who's that?"

I said, "Mimi Howlett."

He said, "I knew Mimi when she was an editorial assistant," and right away I thought, *He slept with her.*

He asked me what the last book I loved was. I was trying to remember the title of any book I'd read recently, when he added, as though it was just another bit of conversation, "Did you read my book?"

"Yes," I said.

"Did you like it?"

"A lot," I said.

He asked if I minded that he'd written a novel about us, and I said, "I minded the way you submitted it to my publisher."

"It was a mistake," he said. "I'm sorry."

"I know," I said.

He said, "I was a little bit desperate."

"Can you be 'a little bit desperate'?" I asked. "Isn't that like being 'a trifle horrified'? Or 'mildly ecstatic'?"

"Leave a man his dignity," he said.

I said, "The amazing thing was that you pulled off a happy ending."

He said, "We deserved it."

"How're you doing on the drinking?" I asked.

He said, "Great," and told me that he'd started taking a drug called Antabuse, which would make him violently ill if he drank. Plus, he'd been to AA. He showed me a white poker chip they'd given him to mark his sobriety. He said he didn't go to the meetings, but he carried the chip around in his pocket all day.

I told him I was happy for him. Then I said, "What do you think they give away at Gamblers Anonymous?"

When he hugged me good night, it was just arms and squeezing, but now the familiar lack of comfort comforted me. I'd once told him that his hugging reminded me of the surrogate wire mothers in the rhesus-monkey experiment; it was more like the idea of a hug than the real thing.

"Archie," I said, "your hugging has not improved."

He said, "Lack of practice."

— • —

He called the next day and asked if I wanted to have dinner.

I confessed that I was criminally behind in my submissions and planned to read my head off.

"Bring them here," he said. "And I'll read my head off, too."

I called home before leaving the office. It was a relief not to pretend to be busy. "You sound good," my father said, and I could hear how pleased he was.

———•———

I sat in Archie's big leather armchair. He stretched out on the sofa. When I started to say something, he said, "No talking in the library," and reminded me that I was there to work.

After a while, he said that he was ordering Chinese, which he called *Chinois,* and what did I want?

I said a librarian's "Sh."

He called and ordered—he knew what I liked, anyway—and when our dinner arrived and we set the dining-room table, we both made a joke of not talking and became our own little silent movie. We exaggerated our gestures and expressions; he held up the chopsticks in bafflement—*What can these be?*—and mimed conducting an orchestra.

Over dinner, he asked how I'd gotten so far behind on submissions.

I hadn't wondered how—it just seemed to happen—but now I tried to think. I told him that I wasn't liking anything I read, which made me think it was me and not the manuscripts. "So I reread everything," I said. "And I can't reject anything." It was the truth, and a relief to know it.

"Did this start after you found out about your dad?" he asked.

I shrugged; it seemed wrong to blame it on that, especially since my father had never used his illness as an excuse.

He said, "It's perfectly natural to doubt your judgment about doubting your judgment."

Back in his den, he said, "Let's see what you're reading."

I handed him *Deep South*. "I don't even know what this is about, except bugs," I said. "I keep rereading the first chapter."

He looked at the first page. "It's about a writer who wants to be the next Faulkner."

"I got that much," I said. "But what if he is the next Faulkner?"

"He ain't," Archie said, turning a page.

"But I can't just say that," I told him. "I think Mimi wants me to write reader's reports."

"These are for Mimi?" he said.

I nodded.

"All of them?"

I nodded.

He looked at me, and I could see that he understood what I hadn't wanted to tell him.

"Write: 'This guy wants to be the next Faulkner, and maybe he is, but I can't get past the first chapter.' "

"That's all I have to say?" I asked. "And I can stop reading it?"

"Yes, dear," he said, handing the manuscript to me. "Let's see the rest."

He read the first chapter of all the manuscripts I'd brought, and said, "Nothing wrong with your judgment." Then he asked why I didn't like each one and, using my words, dictated the note I should write to Mimi.

Without a word about my demotion, he explained nuances of my position in the new H—— hierarchy, describing office politics I'd been oblivious to.

"I should know this already," I said.

"No," he said. "How does anyone learn anything?"

I said, "I feel like I'm Helen Keller and you're Annie Sullivan."

"Helen," he said fondly.

I pretended to sign and mouthed, "You taught me how to read."

He had a barky laugh and I laughed just hearing it.

Then I admitted what a terrible time I was having with Mimi. I told him that she looked at me like she couldn't tell if I was smart or not, and that I actually became stupid around her.

He said, "You have no idea how smart you really are."

I said, "Did you sleep with her?"

He said, "No, honey."

———•———

"These notes are great," Mimi said the next afternoon.

"Thanks," I said.

"But the reader's reports you wrote before were a lot more thorough," she said.

I was about to say, *I'll write reports if you want me to,* but then I pictured having to read the bug novel all the way through. Instead, I repeated something Archie had said: "It doesn't seem like an efficient use of my time."

She looked at me as though I'd spoken without moving my mouth. Then she said, "I guess notes are okay." She dismissed me from her office by saying, "Thanks."

I heard myself say, "No problem," which I'd noticed nonnative English speakers sometimes said instead of *You're welcome.*

—•—

Archie had to go to a dinner party, but he suggested I work in his den. He said, "If you want me to, I'll look over your work when I get home."

I didn't want to go back to Ritaville, and my office was fluorescent desolation. I said, "Are you sure you don't mind?"

He said, "Why would I mind?" He told me that the key was where it always was (in the gargoyle's mouth) and to make myself at home.

I did. I read in the leather armchair, with my feet up. I finished all the submissions I'd brought and wrote notes to Mimi. Then I stretched out on the sofa with the copy of *Loony* he'd given to me.

I woke up to him covering me with the afghan.

"Hi," I said.

"Do you want to wake up and go home," he said in a low voice, "or sleep in the guest room?"

"Guest room," I said.

—•—

Archie told me he was reading a manuscript by a neurologist, and it made him wish he could talk it over with my dad.

They'd met only twice, at my aunt's funeral and then at the shore, a visit that gave new meaning to *long weekend*. What I remembered about it was that Archie had smoked a cigarette on the dock and thrown the butt in the lagoon. I'd looked at him as though he was a terrorist threatening our way of life and said, "We swim in there." My voice sounded as haughty as my mother's had the time a handyman had parked on our lawn, and I'd told her, "You can't expect everyone to know your rules." The whole weekend was like that, hating Archie and then hating myself for it.

What he remembered about the weekend was how much he'd enjoyed sitting on the porch with my dad. They'd talked mostly about publishing and books, and now Archie realized that my father had just wanted to put him at ease. "He was so cordial to me," Archie said. "If that weekend was hard on him, he didn't show it."

I remembered my father's relief at our breakup, though he'd never said a word against Archie.

Archie was watching me. "What did your dad say about me that weekend?"

I said, "He said you were charming," which was true.

——•——

We cracked open our fortune cookies and traded the little slips of paper, as we always had. My fortune was about the value of wisdom over knowledge. His was "Great happiness awaits."

When he took a bite of his fortune cookie, I said, "Don't eat it—Jesus! Now it won't come true!"

And he spit it out in his napkin.

I said, "You know what I've always loved about you?"

"What?" he said, resting his chin on two balled-up fists in imitation of a swooning schoolboy.

"You're willing to swallow your pride to make me laugh," I said. "Or spit it out in a napkin."

———•———

I said, "The good news is that these are the last manuscripts from my archive."

I said, "The bad news is that these are the last manuscripts from my archive."

He said, "Let's go to bed."

III

I once read that no matter how long an alcoholic was sober, as soon as he went back to drinking he would be exactly where he was when he'd left off. That's how it was with Archie and me.

I filled his closet with my clothes. My shampoos and conditioners lined the ledge of his tub. He stocked his refrigerator with diet root beer and carrots.

We ate dinner together every night, out or in.

Before bed, from the upstairs bathroom he'd announce, "I'm taking my Antabuse!"

I didn't know what to say. I tried to think what the

right answer might be. Then, I'd call out, "Thanks," as though I'd sneezed and he'd blessed me.

I knew he wanted to have sex if he put on aftershave before bed. I called it his forescent. The sex itself was manual labor. I was there for what happened afterward— the tenderness that didn't come any other way.

Sometimes, we slept face to face, with our arms around each other; one night I woke up and his mouth was so close to mine I was breathing his breath.

—•—

The only friend I told at first was Sophie, the anti-Archiest of them all. I was afraid to, but she didn't even seem surprised. She said, "Does he make you feel better?"

I said he did.

"He's not drinking?" she said.

I told her about Antabuse and the poker chip from AA.

She looked over at me, and thought. Finally, she said, "But don't give up your apartment, okay?"

I told her that my aunt's apartment wasn't mine to give up, and that it hadn't occurred to me to move all the way in with Archie.

She said, "Call me if it does."

—•—

Archie asked if I'd told my parents about him, and I said I hadn't. "How much longer are you going to keep me in the closet?" he said. "It's dark in here. And I keep stepping on your shoes."

—•—

I was going home to the suburbs for the weekend, and Archie gave me a copy of *Loony* for my father. Then he said, "Let's go."

"Let's go?" I said.

He carried my bag around the corner to Hudson Street and hailed a cab. He actually got in and rode with me to Penn Station. He acted like I was a sailor, shipping out.

While I stood in the ticket line, he went to Hudson News and got Tropical Fruits Life Savers and goofy magazines—*DogWorld*, *True Confessions*, and *Puzzler*—for my train ride. We held hands walking to the staircase for my track. It was hard to go. I said that I worried he'd be lonely. He kissed me and told me not to worry. He said, "I'm the last person you should be thinking about."

———•———

That weekend looked just like the ones I'd spent at home before finding out about my father. But I knew now what was underneath. We had lunch out on the patio. We talked and read. Puttered. We ate dinner by candlelight. We acted like we might go to the movies and never went.

When I woke up on Sunday, my mother had been up for hours, gardening. Over breakfast, she told me she was having the house painted in a few weeks. She showed my dad and me the paint chips, all varying shades of white, and pointed out which white was for which room.

"Alabaster seems too formal for our bedroom," he said, joking.

"It is sort of pretentious," I said. "And coconut for the bathroom? I don't think so."

My mother was good at being kidded; she rolled her eyes in pretend annoyance. Then she said, "I want the house to look its best," with a fervor that stopped me.

My dad heard it, too. "The house looks good now, Lou," he said, to the tune of *This is paint we're talking about.*

I went with him to do errands, and we stopped for fruit and vegetables at what had once been the Ashbourne Mall. Lord & Taylor was now a farmer's market, and the department where I'd bought my first bra now sold organic produce.

In the parking lot, I saw the Ashbourne Witches, a mother and two daughters, who still had long shag haircuts and still drove a rusted red Rambler. They'd terrified and thrilled me as a child, when my friends and I spied on them; the lore was that the Witches returned clothes they'd worn.

He thought it was as funny as I did. He said, "I guess that's the worst thing a suburban girl could imagine."

— • —

It wasn't until just before I left that I remembered to give him *Loony.* I didn't mention that the book was from Archie.

My dad seemed pleased, reading the jacket. He flipped through the first pages, and I saw at the same moment he did that Mickey Lamm had inscribed the book for him. "That was the reading I told you about," I said.

He drove me downtown to the train station. He kept the top down on his convertible but rolled up the windows, so it wasn't too blowy for us to talk. Mostly, he wanted to know about my life in New York. Was it getting any easier with Mimi? What did I like about my job? Was I still considering getting a dog? How was Sophie? Had I met anyone interesting?

——•——

When I got to Archie's that evening, he said, "How'd it go?" I told him that my father seemed pretty good, a little tired maybe, but otherwise his usual self.

Archie was still waiting, and I realized just before he said, "You didn't tell your dad about us?" that he'd expected me to.

That's why he'd had the book inscribed.

I thought aloud why I hadn't; I said something like maybe I was trying to protect my father as he'd protected me.

Archie glared at me. "You're equating me with a fatal blood disease?"

"That's not what I mean." Then I realized the truth: "I wasn't thinking about you," I said. "I was just being with my dad."

He gazed at me. "You've grown up, honey."

It felt good to hear it. I thought maybe he was right. Then it occurred to me that if I really had grown up I wouldn't want to be told.

IV

Mimi came by my office and asked if I was free for lunch, and I said, "Sure." She was in a girlsy-whirlsy mood, and linked arms with me walking to the restaurant.

I felt like I was going to have a great time with her, and I was surprised when I didn't.

She wanted to talk about men—"boys," she called them, regardless of age. All the ones in her life seemed to be in love with her, except maybe her husband. He loved her so much that he hated her.

She told me that she'd recently had dinner with her second husband, a Southerner, who still called her "Sugar-pie." Just as sweet was the author who'd taken her to the Yankees' game last night; she hoped he'd stop by the office today, so I could meet him.

Archie had told me I could probably learn a lot from Mimi, and I wanted to. I looked at her eyebrows; how did she get them so perfect?

I nodded as she spoke, which was all that was re-quired, until she asked me if I was seeing anyone. I said that I was, and when she said, "Who?" I could tell that she already knew. Even so, when I told her, I felt like I'd sold something I should've kept.

After lunch, she said that she was getting her hair col-ored and wouldn't be coming back to the office.

I said, "Your hair is dyed?"

"Colored," she said. "Never say dye."

—•—

Following Archie's advice, I had lunch with an agent I liked. The agent had once worked with Mimi and sang her nickname, "Me-me-me-me."

It was almost three o'clock when I got back. There was a note on my chair from Mimi: "Come visit."

When I went to her office, she didn't offer her perfume.

"Sorry I'm late," I said. "I had lunch with an agent."

Her voice was like dry ice. "If you're going to be late, just let me know, okay?"

"Sure," I said, which came out *shir;* around her I sometimes developed a no-running-water Appalachian accent.

She said, "There's a novel Dorrie acquired that I want you to edit, Jane."

I'd edited a dozen novels by then, but knew I was supposed to be excited and tried to act like I was.

She said, "No one's expecting you to make a silk purse out of a sow's ear."

I said, "So, you're expecting a vinyl purse?"

She said, "Just make it the best sow's ear it can be."

———•———

I thought the novel was silk, as it was. But knowing how Mimi felt about it, I spent a whole week editing the first chapter. Before I went on to the second, I decided to show it to Archie.

He told me that I was hyperediting, treating it as though it was a test.

"It is a test," I said.

"You're thinking about Mimi," he said. "Think about . . ." He turned to the title page. "Mr. Putterman."

As soon as he said it, I knew that he was right and I was glad I'd asked him. I beamed at him.

"You love me," he said. "Don't even try to deny it."

———•———

I got lost thinking about Mr. Putterman; I didn't delete a comma without picturing his reaction and asking myself if it was necessary. I averaged about a page an hour, and the next time I looked at my watch, I saw that I was already forty-five minutes late to meet Archie.

I arrived at the restaurant, saying, "Sorry, sorry, sorry."

Archie didn't seem annoyed. "I was just beginning to worry," he said, "Let's get you something to eat."

Later, though, in bed, he said, "Are you asleep?"

"I *was*," I said, our standard joke.

"You don't want to be late, honey." He smoothed my hair. "It tells the people you care about that they can't count on you. That's not the message you want to give — especially now, with your dad sick."

"You're right," I said. I asked him to help me.

"Just think about the person you're affecting," he said. "Think about Mr. Putterman."

———•———

I met Sophie at Tortilla Flats, where my ex-boyfriend Jamie worked as a bartender—just while he decided whether to open a restaurant of his own, direct movies, or apply to medical school again. We were friends now, though I hadn't seen him since I'd gone back to Archie. When I told him I had, his face didn't change. Then he looked at Sophie with an expression that said, *Look out for her.* And she shrugged, *I'm doing the best I can.*

At the table, she and I talked about everything but Archie, until our second round of margaritas.

"Since you haven't brought up sex," she said, "I'm assuming there hasn't been a miraculous improvement."

I said, "It doesn't feel like a problem the way it used to."

"That is a problem," she said.

———•———

Archie and I went up to his farmhouse late Friday night. I was sleepy, but I stayed awake to talk to him while he drove. He didn't ask me to play the old car games— Capitals, Presidents, Twenty Questions, or Ghost—which collectively revealed my lack of knowledge on every subject.

Instead, he asked quizlike questions about my father: what trait I admired most in him (equanimity); what expression he'd said to me most while I was growing up ("Don't take the easy way out, Janie"); what my earliest memory of him was (sitting on his shoulders during a parade).

When Archie said, "We'll have our own little girl one day," my eyes went wide in the dark.

———•———

We woke up to chilly rain. We ate breakfast at the diner and then wandered around town. I went into Fish 'n'

Tackle, thinking I'd make earrings out of lures, but they were all too shiny or feathery, too lurey.

In the afternoon, Archie lit a fire. I read Mr. Putterman. He read Mickey's new book. By early evening, we were both restless.

He said, "Why don't we go out for dinner and a movie?"

I said, "Methinks a better plan was never laid."

He suggested asking Caldwell, his professor friend, to join us. I made a face.

"You look like Elizabeth when she was thirteen," he said.

I said, "Caldwell seems about a hundred and thirteen."

"Don't be ageist," he said.

"He has a bad personality," I said. "He interrupts."

"He's fascinating if you get him talking about Fitzgerald," Archie said. "He wrote the best book on Scott in the field."

I said, "I'll read it."

He shook his head.

"He never asks me questions," I said. "It's like he can't even see me. I'm just your young thing. I'm just the blurry young person sitting across the table."

He kissed me and said, "You are a blurry young person."

V

I planned to spend the long July Fourth weekend with my family instead of with Archie and felt guilty about it.

I told him, but it came out so jumbled he thought I was inviting him to the shore with me.

"It should just be your family, honey," he said, and offered to lend me his car so I wouldn't have to take the bus.

"Thanks," I said, and told him that my brother was driving down from Boston and picking me up. But I pictured my parents' reaction to Archie's white Lincoln Continental pulling into their driveway.

—•—

"I'm trying to think how to tell my dad about us," I said.

"How about this," he said, and imitated me: " 'Good news, Papa! I'm with that charming fellow Archie again!' "

I didn't answer.

"What?" he said. "You think I'm *bad* news?"

I said, "If Elizabeth was going out with some guy who was twenty-eight years older, tell me you wouldn't be upset."

"Your father knows me," he said. "I'm not just some guy who's twenty-eight years older—at least that's not the way I see myself."

—•—

I didn't know how my father saw Archie.

A few months after Archie and I had broken up, my mother mentioned a friend whose daughter was involved with an alcoholic. My mother pronounced *alcoholic* like it was an on the same cell block with *rapist* and *murderer*, and meant crazy and violent and *lock the door.*

My father didn't say anything, and it occurred to me

that he knew, or at least suspected, that Archie was an alcoholic.

—•—

Friday evening, I took my duffel bag downstairs and dropped it by the door. Archie was reading in the den. I leaned over and kissed him and said, "I should take off."

He seemed confused. "Is your brother here?"

"No," I said. "He's picking me up at my apartment."

"Why?" he said. "Why isn't he picking you up here?"

"Honey," I said. "You know I haven't told my family yet."

"Jesus," he said. "Not even Henry?"

He shook his head and went back to his book. He turned the page, though I knew he wasn't reading.

I stood there, waiting for him to talk to me. When I looked at the clock, it was already seven, which was when my brother was supposed to pick me up.

"I don't want to keep you," Archie said, and his voice was mean.

I said, "I was just trying to think of Mr. Putterman."

He said, "I'd like to be Mr. Putterman once in a while."

I said, "You'll have to stop being Mr. Motherfucker first."

VI

I was anxious in the cab. It was almost seven-thirty when I got to my apartment, but there was no sign of Henry. No note on the door. No message on the machine.

I called the shore and told my mother we'd be late,

and she said her usual, "Don't worry, whatever time you get here is fine."

I looked out my window down at Eleventh Street. I watched a young family packing up their huge jeep and leaving for the weekend. I suddenly got scared about how sick my father might be, and how little time I might have to spend with him. I thought, *Whatever time we get there is not fine.*

I decided I'd talk to Henry about being late. But when he finally arrived, he had a guest with him, Rebecca.

We didn't talk at first because Henry had the AM radio on for the traffic report. He said along with the announcer, "Ten-Ten WINS Radio, you give us twenty-two minutes, we'll give you the world."

Outside the Holland Tunnel, Rebecca turned around in her seat to talk to me, and I saw that she was pretty, though you could tell she didn't think about it. She was husky with brown skin, large dark eyes, and a tiny gold dot in her nose. She told me she was a landscape painter who sold water purifiers to pay her rent.

When she said, "You should get one," I thought she'd caught me staring at her nose dot. But then she told me that the water in New York was even worse than Boston's as far as chlorine, lead, and particulates were concerned.

VII

In a few hours, we were on Long Beach Island, driving past the Ocean View Motel, Shore Bar, Bay Bank, Oh

Fudge!, and the frozen-custard stands with their blazing signs in yellow or pink. Then there were just houses and a long stretch of darkness until we pulled up to the pine trees that hid our house from the road.

My father had replaced my mother's antique, practically lightless lanterns with floodlights, and the path was incredibly bright. For a moment, I forgot about my dad's illness and was just glad to be home; walking into the glare of the floodlights, I made my usual joke, "At-ti-ca! At-ti-ca!"

Inside, the three of us were drive-dazed. We stood in the kitchen. Henry opened the refrigerator.

My father came out in his pajamas and seersucker robe. He kissed my brother and me, and told Rebecca he was glad to meet her. He looked a little pale, but I reminded myself that he hadn't been able to play tennis since he'd had shingles.

My mother appeared in her bathrobe, her hair flattened on one side and poofed out on the other. In a sleepy voice, she asked if we'd like cold chicken, which was what she always offered.

Henry and I split a beer, and Rebecca said she'd just have water, which naturally led to the topic of water purifiers. Even though it was after one o'clock, she attached one to our tap to show us how great they were.

My father was coughing, and I worried that he had another bronchial infection. Then I worried about him seeing me worry. I got him a glass of water and one for myself.

Rebecca watched us drink. "It tastes better, doesn't it?" she asked.

My father seemed to be considering.

"It's triple-filtered," she said.

I admitted that I'd forgotten to taste it.

She said that I might not be able to detect the difference anyway, because cigarettes had probably killed my taste buds.

I said, "I thought the whole point of water was that you didn't taste it."

Henry looked at me. " 'The whole point of water'?"

I got fresh towels for Rebecca and showed her to my room. We'd dismantled the bunk-bed complex a few summers ago, but the room was still tiny, and it seemed even smaller now that I had to share it with Rebecca.

I went out to the deck for a cigarette. I'd smoked outside ever since my father had quit, years ago; I was half acknowledging that I shouldn't smoke, half pretending that I didn't.

The houses across the lagoon were dark. Now that Loveladies had been built up, it felt less like the seashore and more like the suburbs. There was no more marshland, no more scrub. It was just big house, pebble yard, big house, pebble yard.

Back inside, Henry had the TV on and a seventies movie had taken over the living room.

I said, "Henry, do you have to watch now?"

"Yes," he said, playing air guitar to the chase music. "I absolutely have to watch now."

For a minute, I got absorbed in the movie—sexy girls vavooming on motorcycles down Main Street.

"Listen," I said, "I want to talk to you."

He began air-guitaring again and gave me a goofy smile.

"I think you should try not to be late so much," I said. "It tells people they can't count on you."

"There was traffic," he said, and turned back to his movie.

I knew my speech lacked the power Archie's had, but I went on anyway. "We want Dad to know he can rely on us."

He turned and looked at me, and I thought maybe he was considering what I'd said. "Why don't you just say you're mad I was late?"

Then Rebecca walked in. "What's on?" she asked.

"It's either *Chopper Chicks in Bikertown*," he said, "or *Biker Babes in Chopperville*."

She sat down beside him. "Groovy."

———•———

Her bed was made when I woke up. Henry was in the kitchen, shaking an orange-juice carton.

"Where's Rebecca?" I asked.

He told me that she was at the wildlife refuge, painting.

"She's just using you for your landscape," I said.

Sounding like myself at twelve, I said, "Is she your girlfriend?"

He shrugged.

I said, "Why did you bring her if she's not your girlfriend?"

"She's funny," he said. "And I thought it would be easier with more people around."

I said, "Easier for who?"

"Everybody."

I said, "*You* don't have to sleep with her."

"Yeah," he said, smiling. "Gross."

I said, "Does she even know about Dad?"

He said, "Of course not."

—·—

Henry and my mother went sailing, and I stayed behind on the porch with my dad. He read a book about how the atom bomb was made. I edited Mr. Putterman.

After a while, I said, "I have a question."

He nodded.

"How come you never told anybody about being sick?"

"It was selfish," he said. "I didn't want to think about it any more than I had to."

I said, "I'm asking so I don't do whatever it was you wanted to avoid. The reason you didn't tell people, I mean."

He smiled at me. "Well put."

Then he took his glasses off and cleaned them, which

was what he did when he was organizing his thoughts. He told me that the main reason was that he didn't want people treating him like a sick person instead of who he was.

That's what made me tell him about Archie.

He didn't seem upset. He told me he was glad I had someone to lean on. That was important, he said.

Then he went back to the bomb, and I to Mr. Putterman.

— • —

We had dinner on the porch, steamed lobster and mussels, white corn on the cob, tomatoes, and fresh bread.

Rebecca was back by then, washing up for dinner.

Henry sat next to me at the table. He nodded at the bowl of mussels and said in a low voice, "Vaginas of the sea." I looked at them and saw what he meant.

My mother served. "Everything's local except the lobsters," she said.

"The mussels are local?" Rebecca said. "Is the water here really that clean?"

"I'm sure it's fine," my mother said in a breezy voice.

She passed the bowl of little vaginas to me, and I said, "No, thanks."

"Jane." My mother was annoyed. "The mussels are delicious."

We stopped talking for a few minutes, and there was only the sound of cracking shells and then my father's cough, and I wondered if this was why my mother was tense. "Great corn," I said to her.

My father asked how Rebecca's painting had gone, and she said, "Great."

"I'd love to see," my mother said.

Rebecca said, "When I finish it."

After dinner, my father said he was tired. My mother followed him into the bedroom, and I heard her say, "Marty? Can I get you anything, sweetheart?"

VIII

I woke up early. I found my mother crying in the kitchen. She'd always been a big weeper; there were balled-up Kleenexes in the pockets of every one of her bathrobes and coats. In the past, I'd teased her about it. We all had. But now I thought of the times she must have been crying about my father and couldn't tell anyone about it. I put my arms around her.

She said that my father had a high fever and his cough was worse; he was talking to Dr. Wischniak on the phone now.

As I got dressed, I could hear him in the next room, not words, but the tone; he spoke as though consulting another doctor about a patient they had in common.

When my mother told me that Dr. Wischniak wanted them to go back to Philadelphia to get an X ray, I said, "I'm going to wake Henry."

She didn't answer.

I said, "I think he'd want me to."

"Okay," she said, though I could tell she wished I wouldn't.

We had breakfast out on the porch. Henry entertained us with stories about his boss, Aldo, who was a great architect from Italy. Aldo kept opera playing in the office all day, which Henry said made everything seem grand and dramatic.

To demonstrate, Henry composed an opera about calling his mechanic: "The transmission?" he sang in a baritone. "No! No! No! That cannot be!"

My father urged me to stay at the shore and enjoy the rest of the weekend. "I'm going with you," I said. "You need me to drive."

He said, "Mom can drive me."

I said, "Has Mom driven you anywhere lately?" I reminded him that she drove the car like it was a bicycle, pushing the gas, then coasting until she slowed down, then the gas again.

"Oh, stop," my mother said.

She was showing Henry what was in the refrigerator for lunch and dinner when Rebecca came into the living room.

"Dr. Rosenal isn't feeling well," my mother explained to her. "I think he'll be more comfortable at home."

"Did he eat those mussels?" she asked.

My mother said, "It is not the mussels."

I felt sorry for Rebecca then, being in our house and not knowing what was really going on.

At the door, my father shook Rebecca's hand and said, "I hope I'll have a chance to see you again."

For a second, I thought he meant, *If I live,* but then I snapped out of it. "Me, too," I said. "Thanks for the great water."

Henry said, "Call me."

———•———

The X ray was clear, but Eli—Dr. Wischniak—had a tank of oxygen delivered to our house, just in case. It was the size of a small child, and stood by the bed.

My father seemed glad to be at home, in the suburbs. The house was old stone and sturdy, cool inside and pretty. Because they'd lived there for so many years, they had everything just as they wanted it. As soon as my father got into bed, under the fresh white sheets and blue cotton blanket, he seemed better.

I said so to my mother.

"I'm so glad I had the house painted," she said. "I think it really makes a difference."

"It does," I said, though I wasn't sure exactly what I was agreeing with.

———•———

By dinner, my father's fever was down, and he was making jokes. When he took a sip of water, he said, "Louise, this water isn't triple-filtered."

I rented the kind of action-adventure movie he liked. In the middle, Henry called. My father motioned for me to stop the video, and as I did, I said, "Freeze, asshole."

My dad exhaled a little laugh.

When I got on the phone, Henry said, "Is Dad really okay?"

"He really is," I said.

IX

Before bed, I called Archie. He didn't answer. For a second, I worried that he was drinking. But it was the Fourth of July, and I reminded myself that he'd said he might go to Mickey's roof to see the fireworks. Or he could be napping. Maybe he went out for a walk. But I caught myself on that one; Archie didn't take walks.

————•————

On the train to New York, I tried to remember the last time I'd heard him say, "I'm taking my Antabuse!" I realized that I'd never actually seen him swallow a pill.

I went to my aunt's apartment instead of his. It was musty, and I opened all the windows. Then I went into my aunt's study and called him.

I listened for alcohol in his voice, but I didn't hear any. I repeated what my father had said about being glad I had Archie to lean on, and he said, "Told you."

I hadn't brought up drinking since he'd told me he'd quit. I felt like I couldn't, which seemed to prove its proximity. I said, "You didn't drink while I was away, did you?"

"If you have to ask," he said, "don't ask." Then: "I don't think I've given you any reason to doubt me."

"That's true," I said.

"Well," he said, "get over here." And I went.

X

I finally finished Mr. Putterman and read it over one more time, thinking of it as the test it was. Afterward, I realized I was more nervous about Archie's reaction than Mimi's, which seemed wrong. I decided to give it to her, without showing Archie first.

She read it overnight, and called me into her office the next afternoon. She held up her perfume and I submitted my wrists.

"This is really fine work, Jane," she said.

I said, "Thanks."

"Where's the letter?" she said.

"The letter?"

Slowly, she said, "The letter to Putterman."

I thought, *You even want me to write the letter you'll sign?*

She went on explaining that the letter to the author should describe the changes "we'd" made to the novel, as well as "our" enthusiasm for the project.

"Almost finished," I said, and took the manuscript back.

———•———

Really fine work, I said to myself on my way home to Archie's. *Really fine work.*

After dinner, I gave the manuscript to him to read. He

took it right up to his study. When he came down, he said, "It looks good, honey."

I said, "I need to know if you think I will ever be really good at this."

He seemed to be considering.

I said, "I need to know if you think I can ever be a fucking great editor."

"Yes," he said. "I think you are fucking a great editor."

I glared at him. There were a dozen cruel remarks I could've made.

He said, "Your aunt Rita always said that the best editors were invisible." Editors worked behind the scenes, he said; it wasn't a job you did for praise or glory—that belonged to the writer.

"You get glory," I said.

"Inadvertently," he said.

I said, "Isn't that what you'd call 'understated self-inflation'?"

He looked at me.

I said, "I don't think there's anything wrong with glory."

He said, "Join a brass band."

"Shut up," I said.

"Snappy retort," he said, and got up to do the dishes.

— • —

In bed, in the dark, he whispered, "I'm sorry I was so hard on you." Then: "You need approval a little too badly, honey."

"I know," I said.

He said, "But you really did do a fine job for old Mr. Putterman."

I said, "Mimi said, '*Really* fine.' "

He turned and faced me. "You gave it to Mimi before showing it to me?"

"Yes," I said.

He sat up and turned his back to me, and lit a cigarette. "Why would you do that?" he said, and his tone put me in the third person.

"What you said—I need your approval too much." I lit a cigarette myself and said, "I was relying too much on your judgment."

I could tell how angry he was by how he smoked— deep drags with too brief intermissions. "I rely on *your* judgment," he said. "I ask you to read *my* editorial letters."

"You don't need me to, though," I said.

"Of course I do," he said.

I said, "But if I wasn't around to read them, you'd be fine."

He said, "You planning on going somewhere?"

—•—

Mimi called me into her office. "You did a wonderful job on the novel," she said. "But I am a little surprised that it took you as long as it did."

"Oh," I said. I thought of the time my Girl Scout leader told me that I hadn't earned enough badges; she'd said, "You have to work at scouting, Janie."

Mimi said, "I didn't mention it yesterday because I didn't want to diminish the work you'd done. I probably wouldn't mention it at all," she said, "if you didn't also take so long reading submissions."

She was looking at me and I knew that she was expecting a pledge of future speed.

But I just said, "Yeah." And, "Yeah," again. Even to myself, I sounded like somebody who smoked cigarettes in front of the drugstore all day.

———•———

I was sulking in my office, when my mother called. She never called in the middle of the day, so when she said, "How are you?" I said, "What's wrong?"

She said, "Everything's fine." Then she told me that my father had pneumonia and had been admitted to the hospital.

Mimi told me to take as much time as I needed.

Archie left work and met me at his house. He sat on the bed while I packed. "It's going to be hard in Philadelphia," he said. "I don't want you worrying about us."

In the cab to the station, he told me that when he was growing up he'd see a look of pleasure cross his mother's face and ask what she was thinking; she'd say, *I was just thinking of your father.* "That's how I want us to be," Archie said.

I smiled.

"What?"

I said, "I was just thinking of your father."

XI

I asked my mother when Henry was coming. We were in the car, on our way to the hospital.

She didn't answer.

"Mom?" I said.

"Yes?"

"When's Henry coming in?"

She said that he had a wedding to go to on the Cape that Saturday, and he'd come either before or after.

"Are you tired?" I asked.

She nodded.

At red lights, she stopped, coasted, stopped, coasted. I was getting carsick. "Do you want me to drive?" I asked.

"I can drive," she said. But she pulled over and got out, so I could take her place at the wheel.

———•———

My father had plastic oxygen tubes in his nose. He didn't smile when he saw me. "Hello, love," he said.

I bent down to kiss his forehead.

He was in a VIP suite, which had wall-to-wall carpeting, a minirefrigerator, and velvety wallpaper. "This is a brothel," I said.

He said, "Don't tell Mom."

Out in the hall, I saw Dr. Wischniak and asked when my dad would be going home.

He said, "I can't answer that yet."

I said, "Is my father dying?"

He looked at me steadily. "We're all dying, Jane."

———•———

In bed, in my old room, I panicked the way I had as a child when my parents had gone out for the evening and the house seemed unprotected and great danger imminent; I'd picture a lion slinking past the den where the baby-sitter watched television or imagine a murderer lurking outside my open door. I'd whisper, "It's never been anything before."

I said those words now.

———•———

All through the day, my father's doctor friends visited, in their white coats. They sat on his bed and patted the blanket where his legs were. My dad asked them questions about their children—"How's Amy liking Barnard?" or "What's Peter up to this summer?"—trying to make them comfortable.

When he asked how my job was, I said, "Okay."

"Really?" he said.

"No," I said. I told him that I wasn't sure I belonged in publishing. "I'm getting worse instead of better."

"You keep talking about whether you're good at this or not," he said. "The real question is, do you enjoy it?"

"I might hate it," I said.

He reminded me that I loved books.

"I don't read books," I said. "I read manuscripts that aren't good enough to become books."

"What do you think you'd like to do instead?" he asked.

I said that I'd been thinking about writing a series of

pamphlets called "The Loser's Guide." I said, "Like 'The Loser's Guide to Careers.' Or 'The Loser's Guide to Love.' " I wasn't sure whether I was kidding or not.

"Any other ideas?" he said.

I told him about a jewelry store with the sign PIERCING—WITH OR WITHOUT PAIN.

He laughed.

"But I wouldn't want to pierce anything but ears," I said. "Maybe the occasional nose."

———•———

The drugs he was getting made him nauseated, and my mother tried to tempt him to eat. "What about a pastrami sandwich?" she said. "Maybe tomorrow I'll bring a baked potato and a nice steak."

I said, "You always say, 'a nice steak,' like there are also mean steaks."

On our way out to the hospital parking lot, I told her that maybe talking about food while Dad was nauseated wasn't such a great idea.

"He has to keep his strength up," she said.

The way she spoke reminded me more of humming than thinking.

———•———

At home, we had a glass of wine on the screened-in porch, both of us still wearing our visitor tags from the hospital. The sky was the dirty violet of rain coming.

I tried to bring up topics other than my father. I asked about the neighbors I remembered. "How's Willy Schwam?" He had a scholarship to Juilliard. "What happened to Oliver Biddle?" His father died; mother and son moved to Florida.

The Caliphanos lived there now; they were raising their granddaughter, Lisa, because Lisa's mother was a drug addict. She was a serious little girl, my mom said, adorable in braids; she'd knocked on the door last week and said, "I have a feeling there are rabbits in your backyard."

"What did you say?" I asked.

"I said, 'Let's go see.' "

My mother told me about all the neighbors, going up one side of the street and then the other. After she went upstairs to bed, what stayed with me wasn't the good news—weddings or babies or scholarships— but the Caliphanos' granddaughter living without her mother, Mr. Zipkin losing his job, and Mrs. Hennessy getting robbed. I sat out there on the porch, with a cigarette and another glass of wine, listening to the crickets and the occasional car. It occurred to me that the quiet in the suburbs had nothing to do with peace.

XII

Over the weekend, my father told me he was concerned about my missing work; when was I going back?

"I'm taking a leave of absence," I said, deciding then. "I'm malingering vicariously through you."

He said, "I'm glad."

Then he looked right at me, and said, "It means a great deal to me that you're here."

—— • ——

My mother said that there was no reason for Henry to come, as long as I was here. But I kept expecting he would, and Archie did, too. "Stay as long as you need to," Archie said, "but don't forget I need you here."

—— • ——

One night, Archie told me I sounded vague.

I said that it was the suburbs. "They put tranquilizers in the water."

My mother was standing there, and smiled.

"Honey," he said, "I'm not getting a clear idea of what's going on down there."

I tried to explain, but I realized I wasn't sure myself. So I called Irwin Lasker, one of the doctor friends who visited every day. Dr. Lasker was gruff and his sarcasm had frightened me as a child, when I'd been friends with his daughter and slept over at their house.

"The doctors are telling you what you need to know, Jane," he said, and he sounded angry. "It's up to you whether you want to listen or not."

I got angry myself. "Maybe when you hear about blood counts you get the big picture, but I don't."

He didn't speak right away, and when he did he was grave, and I realized I'd asked him to imagine his own daughter hearing about him. "It's just a matter of days, Jane."

When I told my mother what he'd said, she cried, and then she got angry at Dr. Lasker.

"Mom," I said, "I asked him to tell me."

She said, "Irwin's a pessimist."

———•———

The next morning, her eyes were so swollen from crying that they were almost closed. I got her to lie down and brought her ice cubes in a washcloth and cucumber slices. We waited to go to the hospital until the swelling went down.

She put on her prettiest summer dress. This was her way of making my father feel that she was okay. But it was something else, too. It was almost a superstition—like if she looked pretty enough everything would turn out well.

I didn't know what I looked like. I was seeing myself in the mirrors of my adolescence, where I'd discovered that I'd never be a beautiful woman. It mattered to me less now than it ever had, but when my mother said, "Put on a little rouge, Jane," I did.

She watched me anxiously, and I said, "You look like you could use a tall glass of suburban water."

She nodded, not getting my joke. She stood in the doorway in her pretty floral dress, a watercolor of her former self.

XIII

As a doctor, my father must have known what was happening. It may have been gradual but it seemed to me that all of a sudden he became very quiet. When his friends visited, he answered their questions, and that was all.

———•———

I worried that he was thinking about dying, but I wasn't going to bring it up; I asked if there was anything on his mind.

"Yes," he said. "How's it going with Archie?"

"Pretty good," I said.

"Good," he said.

"I know you were relieved when I broke up with Archie last time," I said. "Will you tell me why?"

He said that he'd noticed Archie's insulin in the refrigerator at the shore that weekend. "Diabetes is a serious disease," he said. "But he didn't treat it like it was. He wasn't taking care of himself, which made me think someone else would wind up doing it. His daughter didn't seem to visit or feel much of an obligation to him. I worried that you'd be the only one. I didn't want you to spend your life that way." He paused. He asked me if I knew how long Archie had been diabetic—an important prognostic factor, he said.

I said I didn't. Archie's standard line was that Beefeaters had eaten his pancreas.

I must have looked worried, because my father said, "It's hard, isn't it, love?"

I said it was.

———•———

I began to notice how formal he and my mother were. She spoke to him in a soothing voice, but distantly, and he was just as cool. He acted as though dying was his own private business, and I guess it was.

——•——

Walking back with my mother to the car, I said, "Wasn't it hard keeping Dad's illness a secret all those years?"

She looked at me as though I'd accused her of something.

"Did you and Dad talk about it a lot?"

She said, "At first we did." Then she told me that she'd cried to him once about how scared she was; he'd told her that he could not comfort her about himself.

I said, "Did you ever want to talk to anybody else about it?"

"No," she said. "It was between your father and me."

——•——

My mother told me that Henry might not come down this weekend as planned; his firm was entering a competition and Aldo had asked him to draw the trees—a big honor.

I realized how angry I was that Henry wasn't here, and I called him right back and said, "You should come right now."

"That's not what Mom said." He told me that it wasn't just the competition, he wanted to research the newest treatments for Dad's disease; he'd read about one in Scotland, but so far they'd experimented only on mice.

"Mice?"

We had to be open-minded, Henry said; we'd given conventional medicine a chance and it wasn't working. In a different voice, he said, "I can't just sit around waiting for Dad to die."

"Henry," I said, "Dad isn't going to Scotland."

"Maybe we'll have to force him," he said.

I was about to say, *Force Dad?* Instead, I took a breath. "Please come," I said. "I need you here."

After I hung up, my mother avoided looking at me. I said, "What do you think I did that was so wrong?"

"I didn't say you were doing anything wrong," she said, in the even tone she now used with my father.

I said, "You're not talking to me anymore."

"That's not true." She turned her attention from the dishes to the stove and back to the sink.

"Mom," I said, "you look at me like I'm the enemy of hope."

"Sweetheart," she said. Her voice was creamy. "This is hard on all of us."

———•———

Henry arrived the next morning.

At the hospital, he took over, talking to the doctors and the nurses. He reminded me of my father in an emergency; he was calm, getting all of the facts.

We went into my father's room together. He was sleeping. My mother was sitting by the bed, and Henry put his arm around her, which I'd never seen him do before. I was grateful to him for that.

My mother wasn't angry that he hadn't come sooner, of course. I didn't think my father was either. After all, Henry had done as he was told.

———•———

At home, in the kitchen, Henry and I split a beer.

"Oh," he said, and he took a gadget out of his bag. I recognized one of Rebecca's water purifiers. He attached it to our tap, and then ran the faucet. He handed me a glass, and got one for himself.

"It tastes the same to me," I said.

He said, "Your taste buds are dead."

In a Southern accent, I said, "That girl is a waterhead."

He said, "I like her." Then: "When'd you get back with ol' Archie?"

"I don't know," I said. "May?"

He nodded. I steeled myself to be teased, but Henry just said, "Ready?" and turned off the kitchen lights.

———•———

In the middle of the night, the phone rang.

I sat up in bed not breathing right and waited for my mother to come into my room.

"Jane," she said, at my door. "It's for you."

I followed her to the phone. It was New York Hospital. Archie was in intensive care.

X I V

I took the first train to New York in the morning.

At the hospital, I was told that Archie had been moved from the ICU to a regular room. He was asleep, so I went into the hall and asked the resident what had happened.

She told me that he'd been admitted with severe front-to-back abdominal pain, dizziness, shortness of breath, intense thirst. Then she spoke in the medical language I'd become accustomed to not understanding.

I interrupted and asked what had brought this on.

She said that he had a flu and because he wasn't eating, he hadn't taken his insulin, which was a big mistake.

"But nothing about drinking?" I asked.

She said, "I haven't spoken to him myself."

When I went back into the room, Archie was up. "I thought you needed a vacation," he said, trying to smile. "But it's kind of a busman's holiday."

I said, "I hate buses."

He said, "I have acute pancreatitis."

"I thought it was just average looking." I looked up at his IV. "What're you drinking?" I asked.

He said, "I'm sorry you had to come." Then he fell asleep again.

———•———

I went to the pay phone and called my father's hospital room in Philadelphia.

"What's going on there?" he asked.

I told him what the resident had said about the flu and insulin. My father said, "He went into DKA, diabetic ketoacidosis," and explained what it was so that I understood.

I was relieved to hear him sounding like himself. "Sweetheart," he said, "this was what I was talking about."

"I know," I said.

Then he said, "Did the resident say anything else?"

I said, "Something about acute pancreatitis."

He was quiet a second. Then he said, "Is Archie an alcoholic, Jane?" He sounded as though he already knew.

I didn't want to answer, but I said, "Yes."

His voice was gentle. "We'll talk about that when you come back." Then he said, "He's on an IV, getting sodium and insulin?"

"Something clear," I said.

He told me that Archie would be fine.

I said, "How are you, Papa?"

"About the same," he said.

I said, "I'll come as soon as I can." And he didn't argue.

——•——

I met Archie's real doctor in the hall.

"You're Jane?" he said.

I nodded.

"Okay," he said, "now listen to me." I couldn't tell whether he was furious or just in a rush. *Did I know how serious this was?* He told me that Archie could've lapsed into a coma and died. The doctor seemed to hold me responsible: I needed to regulate his diet and exercise; I needed to be vigilant about monitoring his blood sugar.

I said, "You better talk to him."

He said, "I'm talking to you." Then he walked away.

——•——

I sat by Archie's bed and repeated what his doctor had told me. I said, "He wants me to boss you around."

"We'll pick up a pair of stilettos on the way home," he said.

I said, "I need to go back to Philadelphia."

"Your mother's there," he said.

I told him that Henry had finally arrived, too.

"So, can't you stay?"

"No," I said.

"Jesus," he said. "Not even one goddamned day?"

"My father's about to die," I said. "And you're about to get better." I asked him who I could get to help us out, and as I said it I realized how few friends Archie seemed to have.

"Call Mickey," he said.

"Isn't he kind of clownish for this situation?"

"This situation calls for a clown." He hummed "Send in the Clowns."

—•—

Mickey arrived, wearing cutoffs and yellow high-tops. He was unshaven, and his hair looked greasy. He bent down and kissed Archie's cheek.

Archie made a face.

"I'm sorry I have to go," I said.

Mickey said, "I'm going to steal some drugs," and went into the hall.

I could see how hard it was for Archie to say, "Stay just a little longer?" and I took a later train back to Philadelphia.

XV

When Henry picked me up at the station, he told me that Dad was on a respirator now and heavily sedated. He was being kept alive, but that was it.

At the hospital, the respirator made a big inhale-exhale sound, breathing for my father. I held his hand. But I couldn't tell if he was still in there.

The nurse came in with a square plastic bag of blood. "He knows you're here," she said to me. "I can tell by the monitor." Then she turned to him. "I'm giving you some red cells now, Dr. Rosenal."

——•——

Henry called friends and relatives, and they started coming.

——•——

Once everyone had left, I sat in the chair beside my father's bed again. I thought of Kafka's story "The Metamorphosis," and how Gregor's sister knew to feed him garbage once he'd become a cockroach.

I tried to explain to Henry that this was the transcendent act I wanted to do now.

He said, "Please don't feed Dad garbage."

"I don't know what Dad wants me to do," I said. "I just know I'm not doing it." Henry took my hand and held it.

——•——

My father died later that night.

X V I

I called Archie at home. He said all the right things, but I didn't really hear any of them. He asked when the funeral was, and I told him.

"Do you want me to come?" he said.

"No," I said, "I'm fine," as though answering the question he'd asked.

———•———

Sophie drove down. She stayed with me in my room, and scratched my back while I talked.

———•———

My mother's mother didn't come to our house until the funeral. She spoke to the caterers. She looked over the trays of meat and salads that would be served after the funeral when people would come back to the house. She clicked around the kitchen in her high heels and talked to my mother about who was coming and how many people and—*Remember Dolores Greenspan? She called.* I thought that maybe my grandmother couldn't bring up my father. But then I realized that she was trying to help: make everything appear fine and sooner or later it would be. This was what she'd taught my mother.

———•———

My mother, Henry, and I got into the black limousine that had come to take us to the funeral. When a woman I didn't recognize walked up the driveway, Henry said, "Who's she?"

My mother said that she was a neighbor who'd offered to stay here during the funeral, when burglars might come, thinking the house would be empty. "Mrs. Caliphano," she said to me.

The woman waved, and my mother nodded.

"She seems like a nice lady," my brother said. "I hope they don't tie her up."

———•———

The night before Henry went back to Boston and I to New York, I told him that I hated to think that Dad was worrying about me when he died.

"He wasn't worried," Henry said.

"How do you know?"

"I was there when you called," Henry said. "After he hung up, I said that I'd be happy to kill Archie if he wanted me to. And Dad said, 'Thanks, but I think Jane can take care of herself.' "

XVII

Archie was kind and patient. He kept fresh flowers on the table. He somehow found soft-shell crabs for dinner, even though they were out of season. He drew a bath for me every evening when I came home from work. A tonic for the spirit, he said.

———•———

He invited Mickey to spend Labor Day weekend with us in the Berkshires, maybe hoping to break the spell of my grief.

Mickey told a lot of jokes, most of which were of the animals sitting-around-talking variety, my favorite. He did little comedy bits: after lunch, he turned to me and in a twangy voice said, "I have weird thoughts sometimes. Do you think that's weird?"

It hurt not to laugh. Finally, I asked him to give up on me for a while.

Sunday, when they went to play golf, I stayed behind

at the house. I took the manuscript for Mickey's new book out to the picnic table underneath the apple tree.

I adored Mickey. I thought he was sweet to try so hard to make me feel better. But he irked me that weekend as he never had before. The tiniest things bugged me—like, his not washing his cereal bowl or coffee mug. I even wondered if Archie had noticed—and it bothered me, thinking he hadn't.

Monday night, Archie called Mickey and me in from the meadow, saying, "You kids ready to go?" And I realized that what I'd been feeling that weekend was sibling rivalry.

XVIII

There's a passageway connecting Port Authority to Times Square—the Eighth Avenue subways to the Seventh—and one morning when I looked up I saw a poem up in the eaves, sequential like the Burma Shave billboards:

> Overslept.
> So tired.
> If late,
> Get fired.
> Why bother?
> Why the pain?
> Just go home.
> Do it again.

Something changed then. I saw my life in scale: it was just my life. It was not momentous, and only now did I recognize that it had once seemed so to me; that was while my father was watching.

I saw myself the way I'd seen the cleaning women in the building across the street. I was just one person in one window.

Nobody was watching, except me.

———•———

At the office, Mimi told me that there was another of Dorrie's acquisitions that needed to be edited.

I stood at her desk, looking at the bulky manuscript. "Wow," I said. "This is a long one."

"The author's been calling me and yesterday he called Richard," she said, referring to the editorial director. "So it's sort of a rush."

I didn't pick up the manuscript. I pinged the rubber band. "Did you look at it?" I asked, stalling.

She turned her head—not a no, not a yes. "Jane," she said, "I can get a freelancer. Or do it myself over the weekend. But it would be great if you could help out."

It was hard turning down an opportunity to be great. When I did, I saw her delicate eyebrows go up.

———•———

At Tortilla Flats, Jamie introduced his current girlfriend, a waitress named Petal. She had a little daisy tattoo on her ankle and seemed light and sweet and sure of herself in the particular way a very young woman can.

At our table, I asked Sophie if I was ever like that.

"Like what?" she said.

"Like Petal in any way," I said.

She said, "You used to be twenty-two."

"Jesus," I said, "Jamie must be thirty-five."

"Twisted," she said, and got up to go to the bathroom.

I looked around me. It was Thursday, a party night, and I could feel that bar-generated electricity—the buzz and spark of sex-to-be. Everyone appeared to be having a great time, flirting and drinking and half dancing to R & B, which I loved and never heard at Archie's.

When Sophie returned, I said, "I think being with Archie makes me feel older than I am."

"You do live his way," she said. "It's an older person's life."

XIX

Archie was elated that I felt better.

On our way up to the Berkshires, he asked me to think about moving in with him.

I didn't speak.

He forced a laugh and said, "I didn't mean you had to start thinking about it right this minute."

———•———

Saturday morning, I felt the way I had as a child, waking up in the summer and sensing what I could expect that day in the suburbs: the dry cleaner at the back door to drop off my father's suits; the damp smell of the changing room at the public pool; the dusty shade in the garage.

Maybe Archie could sense it. He suggested we go to the swimming hole, a muddy pond he'd called the Butthole and had refused to go to in our last life. We swam in old sneakers.

On the way home, we stopped at the farm stand for vegetables and fruit. He made dinner and we had a picnic underneath the apple tree in back. He read *Washington Square* to me by flashlight.

When he got into bed and I smelled his aftershave, I said, "Can we just fool around for a while?"

"What does that mean?"

I couldn't think how to say it without hurting him. "Not be so focused on The Problem. You know," I said, "less goal oriented."

"Goal oriented?" he said. "What kind of talk is that? That's like *interact* and *lifestyle*." He turned his back to me. "You know I hate that kind of talk."

In the morning, he wouldn't speak to me. I said, "You're mad just because I used the expression *goal oriented?*"

He said, "I don't like the way you talk to me."

———•———

We drove back to New York in silence.

"Harrisburg, Pennsylvania," I said finally.

He said, "What?"

I said, "I'm willing to play one of your stupid road games, if you want to."

"I don't feel much like playing one of my stupid road games," he said. "But thanks."

On the West Side Highway, he said, "What street are you on?" It didn't seem strange to him that he didn't know.

When he stopped at my building, I said, "I tried to talk to you about something important."

He leaned over me and opened my car door.

I went upstairs into my apartment. It had that unlived-in feel. Dust on my aunt's pictures. No diet root beer in the refrigerator.

I got a bottle of scotch from her liquor cabinet and one of her crystal glasses. I went out to the terrace. It was raining a little. After a few minutes, though, I heard voices coming from the terrace below mine; I saw a tall woman and a shorter man. I couldn't make out words, but they seemed to be having an argument, and I didn't want to hear it.

I went into my aunt's study and sat at the desk where she'd written her novels. I thought I might write something myself. But I wound up just writing what I'd said to Archie and he'd said back.

I got into bed and turned off the light. Lying there, I felt like Archie had sent me to my room.

Then I heard my father's voice saying his usual phrases:
Life is unfair, my love.
I can't make the decision for you.
Don't take the easy way out, Janie.

Then he was gone. The quiet sounded loud. I got dressed and walked to Seventh Avenue for a cab. I let myself into Archie's.

Upstairs, I got into bed with him. He turned away from me. I put my arms around him.

"I'm here about the apartment," I said. "You advertised for a roommate? A smoker who can't name the capitals?"

"I can't talk to you about our problem with sex," he said. "I can hardly talk to myself about it."

———•———

I asked him to tell me the truth about drinking, and he did.

He'd been drinking all along. He told me all the times he could remember. I went back over each one. Then I asked about other times when I'd sensed something was wrong, and went back over the years to the first time — when I'd gone over to his house to tell him that Jamie and I had broken up.

This was how I'd felt finding out about my father; it was like getting the subtitles after the movie.

Archie tried to reassure me. He told me that he was not drinking now, and he swore to me that he wouldn't again. He took Antabuse and kept the poker chip in his pocket. But these had failed him before—or he'd failed them. He would drink again, I knew that. It was part of who he was.

X X

I asked Mimi to have lunch with me. At the restaurant, she told me I needed protein and suggested I order the liver or steak with a good cabernet.

When the waiter came to the table, I told him that I'd have the salmon.

"I'll have the same," she said.

She said that she'd come to this restaurant for lunch alone after her own father had died. "I just sat at the bar and ordered soup." She told me that she was crying when an ex-boyfriend from years before happened to walk in. "He sat down and put his arm around me," she said. "He seemed to think I was still upset about our breakup."

I laughed, and she said, "Boys always think everything is about them."

I thought, *Whereas everything is really about you, Me-me.* But I understood her now as I hadn't before. I understood that she needed to be told who she was. Just as I had.

She said that her father's death had been the hardest thing in her life. "We are all children until our fathers die."

I said, "I feel sort of like an adolescent again."

She gave me a look of older-sister understanding.

"At work, I mean," I said. "I've gone backward. If I keep going this way, I'll be heading down to personnel soon to take a typing test."

She started to disagree, but I stopped her. "I've become your assistant," I said. "I used to be an associate editor."

She said, "That's still your title."

"I need to be one, though," I said. "I'm not asking for a promotion," I said. "I'm telling you that I need to be un-demoted—or else I have to quit."

Her face was even paler than usual, which I hadn't

thought possible. I could see the blue of a vein just under her eye. "You haven't exactly proven yourself."

"I know," I said. "You're right."

"I have to think about this," she said.

I told her I was letting her pick up the check, on the chance that I'd soon be unemployed.

—•—

"You've got balls," Archie said.

"Could you put that some other way?" I said.

He said, "But what if she lets you quit?"

I told him I thought she would. "I don't think I belong in publishing anyway."

"Since when?" he said, strangely.

"I don't know."

He looked at me as though I'd said I wanted to sleep with another man.

"It's all about judging," I said. "I'm not sure I'm the judge type. I might be more of the criminal type."

"Judgment is power," he said.

I said, "I thought knowledge was power."

"Why are we talking like this?" he said.

"You're right," I said. But I told him that I didn't think I wanted power. "I think I want freedom."

He said, "Freedom's just another word for nothing left to lose."

I said, "You're sinking to my level."

—•—

Mimi let me resign. "I feel terrible about this," she said. "Maybe I could help you find another job."

"No," I said. "I'm quitting publishing cold turkey."

She said, "I feel the way I did when my first husband left me."

This was a story I wanted to hear.

"He thought he was gay," she said. "It wasn't enough for him to leave me, he had to leave my whole sex."

"Was he gay?" I asked.

"Of course he was."

I said, "But you said 'he thought he was gay.' "

"I think you're missing my point, Jane."

We agreed that I would leave in two weeks.

———•———

I heard Archie turn the key in the door.

He kissed me and said, "What's the matter?"

"Nada thing," I said. "I was let quit."

He said, "Oh, honey," as though I'd made a terrible mistake.

"Don't say it like that," I said. "I'm about to embark on an exciting career as a temp."

"No," he said, and he snapped his fingers. "You'll come work for me at K———. And be a real associate editor."

I said, "I could bring you up on charges for that."

"What?"

"Work harassment in the sexual place."

———•———

On my last day of work, I went by Mimi's office to say good-bye. "There's something I've been wanting to ask you," I said.

"Of course," she said.

"How do you get your eyebrows so perfect?"

"Carmen," she said, and she wrote down the number of her eyebrowist. Then she sprayed perfume on my wrists one last time, and I was out.

On the subway home, I got a little scared. I remembered the phrase *career suicide*. But then I thought, *Goodbye, cruel job.*

———•———

The following Monday, I went to the temp place. I aced my typing test. I soared through spelling and grammar. I was sent to the benefits department of a bank, where I typed numbers into a computer and answered the phone.

"Today was the first day of the rest of my life," I told Archie when I got home. "It was okay. I think the second day of the rest of my life will be better."

He tried to smile, but it was just a shape his mouth made.

While I was cooking dinner, I found Motown on the radio and danced around the kitchen.

"What is this?" he asked, as though he'd caught me reading a comic book.

I sang along to the music: "I'll take you there."

He said, "I live with a teenager."

"Why are you so upset?" I asked him in bed.

He said, "I don't know," and I realized I'd never heard him say these words before. "I wanted to help you, and now I can't even do that."

"It's better for me, honey," I said, but he didn't answer.

XXI

The next weekend we went up to the farmhouse. He did whatever I wanted to and nothing I didn't. He didn't ask me to play Scrabble or Honeymoon Bridge or Hearts. He didn't suggest we invite the professor over for dinner.

In the late afternoon, he took me to the flea market. He ate hot dogs at the concession stand and read the newspaper while I hunted for treasures. When I showed him what I'd bought—cardboard farm animals with wooden stands—he said, "How did we live without these before?"

———•———

Saturday night, we lay outside on the grass. The moon lit up the meadow and the stars were out. It must've been their brightness that made me remember a radio jingle from when I was growing up, and I sang it to Archie: "Everything's brighter at Ashbourne Mall."

He got the tune right away, and sang, "Ashbourne Mall."

After a while, he said, "Honey."

"Yes, honey," I said.

He put a little box in my hand. I looked at it. It was that robin's-egg blue from Tiffany. I opened the blue box, and there was a velvet one inside, and I opened that. I looked at the ring. It was platinum with one diamond. It was just the ring I would've wanted, if I'd wanted a ring from him.

I said, "It's beautiful."

He heard the remorse in it. "Oh," he said, "I see."

I was about to say, *I can't make a big decision right now—I can barely trust myself to decide what earrings to wear.* But I said, "I'm sorry, honey."

He spoke softly. "I knew you wouldn't marry me when you didn't ask me to the funeral."

My father was gone. I felt I couldn't lose anything else, but just then I realized I already had: I'd lost the hope that I would ever be loved in just that way again.

———•———

I walked through the meadow. I sat at the picnic table. I looked hard at everything, so I wouldn't forget. Then I picked an apple from the tree for the ride home.

In the car, Archie said that it was hard letting me go; I was probably the last shot he'd have to start a new life.

I started to disagree, but he got angry. "Jesus," he said. "At least pretend the idea of me with another woman is still hard for you."

"Harrisburg, Pennsylvania?" I said.

He said, "Albany, New York."

———•———

When he pulled up to my apartment, I said, "You don't want me to come over and get my stuff?"

"No," he said. "I don't."

I was a little afraid of him just then.

Then he reached over and took my hand. We sat like that, in front of my building, for what felt like a long time. Then he hugged me, and said, "My little rhesus monkey."

———•———

Archie waited a week to call me. He said I could come over and get my things anytime I wanted to.

I said, "I'll come over tomorrow morning."

"You don't want me to be here," he said.

"I think it would be easier," I said.

"It shouldn't be easy," he said. I knew he was right, and I was about to say so, when he added, "Don't take the easy way out, Janie."

"You can't do that," I said. "It's a violation of the Versailles Treaty."

"Well," he said, "according to the Geneva Convention, I get to say good-bye to you."

———•———

Instead of taking the key from the gargoyle's mouth, I rang the bell.

He opened the door. "Hello, honey," he said.

"Hi." In the foyer, I saw my clothes and books in beige plastic bags that had once delivered our *Chinois*. My cardboard farm animals grazed on a box of my books.

"Can you stay for a minute?" he said, and I said, "Sure."

I saw white freesia on the dining-room table. He poured a diet root beer for me.

We went to the den, and he sat in his big leather armchair. He said, "I'm afraid Mickey's in shock about us. He said he feels like his parents got divorced."

"I think the important thing is that he doesn't blame himself," I said.

Archie didn't smile. "He'd like you to call him."

"I will," I said.

"He asked me why we broke up, and I couldn't explain it to him."

I was about to say, *Honey,* but I said, "Archie."

"Yes, Jane," he said, hurting me exactly how I'd hurt him.

"Are you asking me to explain?" I said.

"I guess I am," he said.

As gently as I could, I told him what I'd figured out about us. He nodded, and I went on, saying what I thought was wrong and why. When I told him that we couldn't talk openly to each other, I realized that I was now. It made me wonder if we really did have to break up.

But then he interrupted: "I guess I don't need to hear all this."

"Okay," I said. "Just tell Mickey we couldn't make each other happy."

He said, "Coleridge said that happiness is just a dog sunning itself on a rock. We're not put on this earth to be happy. We're here to experience great things."

I said, "I don't think you want to tell Mickey we couldn't make each other experience great things."

"Is that what this about?" he said. "Sex?"

"Why are you badgering me?" I asked.

He smiled. "I thought if we had a good fight," he said, "we could make up."

I shook my head, and he stood up, so I could.

He helped me carry the bags outside, and hailed a cab for me.

He said, "You going to be okay on the other end?"

I said I would.

XXII

I saw Archie once more. I spotted him near Sheridan Square, waiting for the light to change with a pretty young woman, pink-cheeked from the cold—a good girl in a camel-hair coat. I couldn't guess her age—I'd lost that ability from being with Archie—but I knew she was even younger than I'd been when we were together. I'd always imagined that he'd wind up with someone closer to his age, just as I would. So it threw me. And for a second, I saw them as the world-weary world did: older man seeks younger woman.

I wondered if they were married. Watching them, I decided they weren't. They were courting each other. Trying to make each other laugh. He had his arm around her, and she was looking up at him. He was a sly boots, but I could tell how badly she wanted his approval. She reminded me of myself, of course.

Crossing the street, he saw me. He smiled, I thought, sadly. It seemed like he might walk past me on the sidewalk, but he stopped, and said, "Hey kiddo," and kissed my cheek.

"This is my daughter, Elizabeth."

I acted as though I'd known who she was.

"Hi," she said. She seemed even younger than her young self, fidgeting with a white mohair glove.

Archie asked me if I was still temping, and I admitted that I was a semi-perm at an ad agency.

She was looking from Archie to me, maybe wondering who I was—or had been—to her father.

I asked how Mickey was. "Tired," Archie said; he'd just delivered his new book.

"The Mickey I met that time?" Elizabeth asked.

Archie said, "Right," and told his daughter and me that the new book, about a baker-bookie, was called *Dough*.

It occurred to me that I would have been Elizabeth's stepmother. I wanted to ask her about herself, what she did and where she lived, but I could see that Archie wanted to go. She could, too, and was taking her cues from him.

She must have felt me watching her walk away, though. At the corner, she turned around and flashed me a gloved peace sign.

I peaced her back. Then they were gone.

YOU

COULD BE

ANYONE

A Girl Scout is clean in thought, word, and deed.

It's easy to be clean on the outside. All you need is soap and water and a scrubbing brush. It's harder to be clean on the inside.

—From *Junior Girl Scout Handbook*

He's broad and muscular from lifting weights and running every evening along the Hudson River. Blond and blue-eyed with a strong jaw and skin so pale it looks bleached. He is all handsome and no pretty, the kind that makes you think of the Navy and Florida and girls in tube tops calling him hunky. But he grew up in Manhattan, on Park Avenue: he will rise when you enter the room; he will notice that you're cold and drape his blue blazer around your shoulders; he will hail the taxi and open the door for you to get in.

On your first date, he will pick you up on his motorcycle, and bring a helmet for you. He nods his big helmet head when he's ready for you to get on. He fastens your hands around his waist like a seat belt.

You sense that he's dangerous but don't know why— and wonder if it's because he makes you feel safer than you've ever felt.

At the restaurant, low-lit and charming, he orders

bourbon straight up with a beer chaser, and becomes low-lit and charming himself. When your dinner arrives, he takes vitamins out of his shirt pocket, and offers a twin supply for you.

You walk through the Village. It's spring. The air is cool and the sky is clear.

Back at your apartment, you pour him a glass of wine. On your sofa, he holds your hand in both of his, tickling and touching it, lingering at the crotches between your fingers.

You can feel that he wants to own you—not like an object but like a good dream he wants to keep having. He lets you know that you already own him.

———·———

He cannot see you often enough. He calls you every day at work, calls you every night at home. He says, "This is your boyfriend speaking."

He invites you to hear his moribund rock band, Pleather, at The Bitter End. The songs are harsh and vulgar, except "Will You Love Me Tomorrow."

He pushes his clothes aside to make space for yours in his closet.

He worries about your riding your bicycle in Manhattan. He buys you a flashing red light to put on your helmet, and when you ride away, he sings, "Staying alive, staying alive."

You love Airedales, and he writes away to make you a member of the Airedale Terrier Society of America. You get a membership card and their monthly newsletter, "The Black and Tan."

He remembers the names of everyone you mention—the people you work with, your friends, acquaintances, your entire extended family—and nicknames them: your complaining cousin Marjorie is "Martyrie"; your boss, Rachel, who has a thing for black guys, is "Racial."

You tell him your family history. He tells you his.

When he speaks of his mother, he uses the ironic intonation of quotation marks: "Mom" still lives in the apartment he grew up in, which he refers to not as home, but by its address. He passes 680 Park five times a week on his way to psychoanalysis.

——•——

You meet a few of his friends from Choate, which he calls "Choke." They banter instead of talk, and you play audience.

"They do shtick," he says afterward. "They're shtick-figures." You wonder at how easily he dismisses them; after all, they've been his friends for almost twenty years.

Then your brother meets him and says, "What's he so angry about?"

That's when you begin to notice. He argues with the drummer in the band. The waiter is rude, the cabdriver an asshole. The token seller gave him a dirty look, the dry cleaner lost his shirts on purpose. He hates our hateful senator, but with passion.

When you mention antidepressants, he looks at you as

though suddenly discovering that you have the depth of a Doublemint twin.

He explains slowly: he wants to use his pain as the impetus and guide in his struggle to know himself; anesthesia is the opposite of what he needs.

You tell him you understand, but say, "Another bourbon and beer?"

———•———

He gets a Polaroid camera and is constantly snapping your picture. In his favorite, you're laughing hard, wearing a pair of his shorts on your head beret-style.

He says that you look like Patty Hearst during her Tanya phase, captured in a lighthearted moment with the Symbionese Liberation Army.

He says he loves the picture because he can see the silver in your fillings.

———•———

In a restaurant, he notices a gaggle of girl models. "It's like looking at art. The rest of us are just people," he says. "We know we're not beautiful the way they are."

———•———

He tells you that he doesn't want to hide anything from you. He wants to be closer to you than he's ever been to anyone.

In this spirit, he confesses the thoughts that shame him. You play the role of Red Cross volunteer, impervious and good-hearted, ladling out mush—until the night he tells you that he has been fantasizing about other women.

You know men do, you would assume that he does, but this truth said aloud, confession-style, becomes your own lurid infection.

He's oblivious. He says, "It's transference," putting himself on the couch: he's hating and loving you the way he did his mother. Fantasies are his way of escaping your power.

When he says that transference is a universal truth, you say, "For you, maybe."

You break up.

—•—

Everywhere you go, you see women more beautiful than yourself.

You imagine him being attracted to them.

You're drinking gasoline to stay warm.

—•—

When he calls and tells you he misses you, you invite him over. He spends the night.

In the morning, he asks where his razor is. You tell him that you threw it away when you broke up. He says, "I framed your deodorant."

—•—

He takes you to Paris for your birthday. Your friends say he's going to propose and you find yourself dressing for the event that you'll both reminisce about years later. You even put makeup on. After a few ringless dinners, though, you stop posing for the memory, and relax. You begin to enjoy the trip, just as he turns black and humorless.

He can't believe how expensive everything is; everyone is so arrogant; he's tired of walking in circles and wonders aloud if there's such a thing as delayed jet lag.

He says, "Are you wearing makeup?"

"You don't like it?"

He says, "I think I like you better without."

In cafés, at museums, over dinner, he barely looks at you, and when he does, it's like he's trying to remember that he loves you.

"What?" you say, finally.

"It has nothing to do with you, honey," he says. "I'm doing the transference dance."

On your last night, after your birthday dinner, he's checking out. You go into his knapsack for a pen and find the engagement ring. You get chills. You lie down. When he comes back upstairs, you say that you're going out for a walk, alone.

"It's almost midnight," he says. "We have to get up early."

"I know," you say.

You walk down to St. Germain to the café where Simone de Beauvoir wrote her letters to Sartre—the café your boyfriend disdained, saying it was full of tourists.

You love it. You order wine. You smoke cigarettes. You play worthy Simone to his unworthy Jean-Paul.

On your second glass of wine, you notice a man staring at you. He's fleshy and balding and has long, straggly hair. You don't realize how short he is until he stands up, hardly rising at all, and comes over to your table.

"Hello," he says, and you see that he's missing one of his front teeth.

He stands before you, and begins to talk. His missing tooth gives him a slight lisp, and you enjoy listening to him. He speaks rapidly, mentioning famous Americans who regularly cross his path. He, himself, is an expatriate from New York; he tells you he's a lawyer, a screenwriter, an entrepreneur, very successful, very rich, and you think, *Hey, why not devote an afternoon and a little cash to getting a new tooth?* But you only smile. He smokes your cigarettes, and you smoke his.

He's entertaining you more than your boyfriend has all week and asking nothing of you, not even to sit down. For a long time, you don't even realize that he's standing, and when you do, you invite him to join you.

You make up a name for yourself, Deena. He is Wallace.

Once seated, he gets personal: "I see you're not wearing a ring, Tina—you've argued with your boyfriend, then?"

"Deena," you say. "I couldn't sleep." You wonder if this sounds credible.

"It's fine if you don't want to talk about it, Deena," he said. "That's fine."

You can tell he has met many women in circumstances like yours, because he speaks in generalities, about freedom and love, passion and fidelity; he's circling above, waiting for a sign from you—yes, that's it, that's my story—so he can land. You remain impassive, though, and finally, he says, "Listen, Tina, this guy has no idea what a remarkable woman you are."

"Deena," you say, adding that if he's going to give personal advice, he should at least get your name right.

"Deena, Tina, Nina," he said, "you know what I'm saying here."

"Yes," you say. "I know what you're saying."

You put some bills on the table for your wine and say you think you can sleep now, not caring if it sounds stagy.

"Listen, Deena . . ." he says, standing as you do.

You thank him for his advice, and before walking out, you bend down and kiss him on both cheeks.

You're a little drunk, but you feel fine. In Motown spirit, you say, "Girl, you can still bring a long-haired shortie with a missing tooth to his feet." You walk several blocks in the wrong direction.

As soon as you enter your hotel room, you're sober and sad again. You undress in the dark and brush your teeth and get into bed.

He says, "I went out looking for you."

You lie there, side by side, in the dark.

You need to tell him that you found the ring, but you hesitate. Telling all is his code. Not telling, however, complies with the code of the Wily Woman.

You say, "I found the ring."

"Fuck," he says.

You say, "You changed your mind about me."

"It isn't you," he says, as though you're to be comforted by the irrelevant role you play in your own life.

He says, "Please tell me how you feel."

You say, "I'm crestfallen," a word you have never used.

"I want to marry you," he says. "I know I do."

He turns on his side and moves closer, and tries to hold you. But you're conscious of his head and his chest and his arms just as hair and skin and bones.

— —•—

The ring stays there, between you.

Sometimes you take it out of his sock drawer and look at it, and try it on. It makes you think of an ad on the back of your old *Seventeen* magazines—a couple in fisherman sweaters with the words, "A Diamond Is Forever."

Even so, you make love before anything else. The few nights you spend apart, he calls to say good night; the next morning he wakes you up by reading Langston Hughes poems on your answering machine.

At Christmas- and Hanukkah- and Kwanza-time, you're blue, because you don't belong to a religion, and his—psychoanalysis—doesn't have any holidays. He makes a candelabra out of wire hangers and duct tape. He lights sparklers and wings a prayer, listing what he believes in—"The Bill of Rights," which he recites from memory, natural-grass baseball diamonds, and your beautiful breasts.

—•—

You notice the swell of one of your breasts, and notice it again weeks later. When you direct his hand to it, his eyebrows slant into worry. He says, "You even swell swell," but he is the one who insists you call your gynecologist in the morning.

She sends you to a surgeon, who doesn't like what he feels. A few mornings later, the surgeon does the biopsy. The pathology lab will have your results in a week.

Meanwhile, your boyfriend reads Dr. Love's book and reports that the odds of getting cancer at your age are almost one in three thousand. He says, "You're not the one."

You keep telling yourself, "This is only a test," but that week of waiting for the results is an unrelieved high-pitched tone. Then you are told that it is a real emergency.

Too late, you realize that your body was perfect—every healthy body is.

After the initial devastation, you're calm. You watch his rage from the eye of your own storm. His "Why you?" seems beside the point, and you say so.

You say, "You're not helping me."

He will make calls, make dinner, make jokes; he will say that a modified radical sounds like a Black Panther who has moved to the suburbs and belongs to a food co-op.

When you decide on plastic surgery to reconstruct your breast, tunneling your latissimus muscle and fat and skin from back to front, he will call it the tunnel of love.

In post-op, he will tell you he is honored that you threw up on him. He will stay with you in the hospital all day, every day, and as late as he can at night. After visiting hours, when the night nurse says he has to leave, he will hide there with you, closing the curtain partition and keeping his feet up on your bed.

He will even get along with your brother. The two of them will take turns reading to you until you fall asleep or the night nurse brings a security guard.

You can feel how much he loves you. For a second, you think maybe if he can just hold on to you like this, he'll keep you from falling off the earth, out of this life.

———•———

After your first chemo treatment, before you lose your hair, he will take you wig shopping. He'll make it fun, and annoy the saleswoman by trying on wigs himself. You get one that looks like the hair you still have, and another like the hair you wished for as a teenager. Long and streaky blonde, it is a wig Tina Turner might have worn in the bad old days with Ike, and he makes you laugh by singing, "Left a good job in the city . . ."

He will buy a satin pillow, which is supposed to slow the breakage and loss of your hair. Maybe it does, at first. Then there's a clump in the drain. A nest in your brush. You see more and more and more of your scalp. You wear a baseball cap all the time, even in front of him—especially in front of him.

When you can't stand it anymore, you ask him to shave your head, and he says he will be honored to be your hairundresser.

He will bring a shaver and temporary tattoos, for what he calls your new headstyle.

The moment before you take off your cap, you cry: "Don't ever remember what this looks like."

"Honey," he says, "I'm the man who loves you."

He sets up two bourbons and two beers, and goes to work. Every few minutes, he turns off the shaver to see if you are okay.

Afterward, the two of you look in the mirror. For less than a second, you see your hideous, hairless self—but right away your survival instinct kicks in and tells you the opposite: you are uniquely beautiful.

When you smile, so does he. "Very cool," he says.

He offers to shave his own head, in solidarity, but you say no. You don't want anyone mistaking you for late-comer disciples of Heaven's Gate; heaven is the last place you want to go, spaceship or no.

He clips pictures of dazzling black basketball players with shaved heads and tapes them to your refrigerator, proof that you belong to the bald beauty elite.

He writes his congressman and Runs for the Cure.

He goes with you to your doctors. He knows all the terminology. He reads all the research. He fills your re-frigerator with grapefruit and oranges, broccoli and carrots. He makes green tea for you. He reminds you to do your visualization exercises.

During chemo, you're more tired than you've ever been. It's like a cloud passing over the sun, and suddenly you're out. You don't know how you'll answer the door when your groceries are delivered.

But you also find that you're stronger than you've ever been. You're clear. Your mortality is at optimal distance, not up so close that it obscures everything else, but close enough to give you depth perception. Previously, it has taken you weeks, months, or years to discover the meaning of an experience. Now, it's instantaneous.

———•———

Two weeks after your last chemo treatment, one week before radiation, you're sitting around your apartment reading the paper, when he says that he feels ready to marry you. "I think I can do it now," he says, passing you the ring box as ceremoniously as if it's the phone, for you.

You don't take it. You say the truth as it occurs to you: "You're talking about you again."

Now he holds the box like it is what it is. "I'm doing the best I can," he says, and you know this is true.

Still, you say, "I'm not sure you even know who I am."

"I'm not sure I do either," he admits.

His words stop you. You realize that if he doesn't know who you are, he won't be able to remember who you were.

When you try to explain, he argues that you're not going anywhere. "Forget dying," you say. "Dying is beside the point anyway."

But then you hear that he can't hear you, you see that he can't see you. You are not here—and you haven't even died yet. You see yourself through his eyes, as The Generic Woman, the skirted symbol on the ladies' room door.

When he says, "I love you, honey," you realize that he never calls you by your name.

You will say good-bye for all the right reasons. You're tired of living in wait for his apocalypse. You have your own fight on your hands, and though it's no bigger or more noble than his, it will require all of your energy.

It's you who has to hold on to earth. You have to tighten your grip—which means letting go of him.

—— • ——

You go through radiation.

Then your immune system is all you have to kill the aberrant cells, which you imagine as sinister and black-clad, smoking cigarettes as they cluster in the dark S & M club of your body.

It was easier when the menace came from the outside, you tell a therapist; she nods, neither agreeing nor disagreeing. Thursday after Thursday, you tell her about your relationship with him. You talk and talk, waiting for the cure. After a while, though, it occurs to you that even a perfect understanding of failed love is the booby prize.

You don't see him again. Sometimes you worry that he loved you better than any man ever has or will—even if it had nothing to do with you. Even now, he is every blue blazer getting into a cab, every runner along the river, every motorcycle coming and going.

THE

GIRLS' GUIDE

TO HUNTING

AND FISHING

. . . [W]hen you're with a man you like, be quiet and mysterious, act ladylike, cross your legs and smile. Don't talk so much. Wear black sheer pantyhose and hike up your skirt to entice the opposite sex! You might feel offended by these suggestions and argue this will suppress your intelligence or vivacious personality. You may feel that you won't be able to be yourself, but men will love it!

—From *The Rules* by Ellen Fein
and Sherrie Schneider

My best friend is getting married. Her wedding is only two weeks away, and I still don't have a dress to wear. In desperation, I decide to go to Loehmann's in the Bronx. My friend Donna offers to come with me, saying she needs a bathing suit, but I know a mercy mission when I see one.

"It might be easier if you were bringing a date," Donna says in the car, on the Major Deegan Expressway. "But maybe you'll meet somebody."

When I don't answer, she says, "Who was the last guy you felt like you could bring to a wedding?"

I know she's not asking a question so much as trying to broach the subject of my unsocial life. But I say, "That French guy I went out with."

"I forgot about him," she says. "What was his name again?"

"Fuckface," I say.

"That's right," she says.

———•———

At the entrance to the store, we separate and plan to meet in an hour. I'm an expert shopper, discerning fabric content by touch, identifying couture at a glance. Here at Loehmann's, on Broadway at 237th Street, I'm in my element—Margaret Mead observing the coming of age in Samoa, Aretha Franklin demanding R-E-S-P-E-C-T in Motor City.

Even so, I search for a whole hour without finding a single maybe, until I see it, my perfect dress, a black Armani sheath—but only in an ant-sized two and a spider four.

I think, A smarter woman than I bought my ten at Saks or Barneys weeks ago, knowing it would never find its way to Loehmann's. She knew her dress when she saw it and didn't hesitate. That woman is zipping up her sheath right now, on her way to meet the man she loves.

But in the communal fitting room, Donna hands me the black Armani sheath in a ten—the one that almost got away. I take this as an omen.

Is the dress perfect? It is so perfect.

I say, "You're my fairy godshopper," and sit on the fitting-room bench, holding the sheath in my arms while Donna tries on bathing suits. She adjusts the straps of a chocolate maillot and frowns at herself in the mirror. She doesn't know how beautiful she is, especially her sultry, heavy-lidded eyes; she says people stop her on the street and tell her to get some rest.

"No wonder I'm single," she says to the mirror. "Even I don't want to get into bed with these thighs."

I say that getting married isn't like winning the Miss America Pageant; it doesn't all come down to the bathing suit competition.

"What do you think it comes down to?" she says.

I say, "Baton twirling."

———•———

Afterward, we celebrate our purchases over turkey burgers at the Riverdale Diner. In a put-on silky voice, I say, "I am a woman who wears Armani."

"Clothes are armor," she says.

I don't need armor, I tell her; I'm happy for Max and Sophie.

"I hate weddings," she says. "They make me feel so unmarried. Actually, even brushing my teeth makes me feel unmarried."

She stops doing her shtick, and suddenly she does look tired; her lids practically cover her eyes. She tells me she's been reading a terrible book called *How to Meet and Marry Mr. Right*. "Their main advice is to play hard to get. Basically, it's a guide to manipulation."

I say that maybe she should stop reading it.

"I know," she says, only half agreeing. "But it's like I've been trying to catch a fish by swimming around with them. I keep making myself get in the water again. I try different rivers. I change my strokes. But nothing works. Then I find this guide that tells me about fishing poles and bait, and how to cast and what to do when the line gets taut." She stops and thinks. "The depressing part is that you *know* it'll work."

I say, "I hate fish."

———•———

The wedding is held at a restored mansion on the Hudson. I come up here sometimes on Sundays. If there isn't a wedding going on, you can pay admission to tour the house and grounds, but I pay my $4.50 just to sit in an Adirondack chair and read the newspaper and look at the river. It's a spot so idyllic that it makes you feel you're in a painting—a Seurat—and for a while I kept hoping a gentleman in shirtsleeves and a boater would dot-dot-dot over to me. Then I overheard a guard say that this place was just for the pinks and grays—wedding parties and senior citizens.

I arrive in the rainy afternoon to help Sophie dress. I'm directed upstairs to the first door on the left, where I expect an old-fashioned bedroom with lace curtains, a vanity, and a four-poster bed, but I find Sophie and her friends in a conference room with stacked plastic chairs and a slide projector. She's at the lectern, clowning in her bra and stockings.

I go up to her and the words *blushing bride* come to mind, though she is, in fact, an almost constant blusher—from sun or wind, laughing, crying, anger, or wine. Now she actually appears to be glowing, and I kiss her and say, "Hello little glowworm."

Her hilarious friend Mavis pours me a big glass of

wine; she's pregnant and says that I have to drink for two now.

After I help Sophie on with her off-the-shoulder ivory gown, she asks me to put on her makeup, though she knows I don't really know how. It's for the ritual of it; I brush a tiny bit of pale eye shadow on her lids and put on barely-there lipstick. She blots her lips with a tissue.

Mavis says, "Jesus, Sophie, you look like a whore."

The photographer knocks to tell Sophie it's time for pictures, and the rest of us follow. Mavis and I stop in the bathroom, and from the stall she tells me she didn't realize for a long time that she was pregnant; she thought she was just getting fat and becoming incontinent. "So the pregnancy was really good news."

Since I have nothing to add about pregnancy, I tell her I read that Tiny Tim wore Depends in his final years. He wasn't incontinent, just thought they were a good idea.

Downstairs, we join Mavis's husband and the other guests. We take our seats in the room where the ceremony will be held. It has a river view, but all you can see now is fog and rain and wet grass.

I ask Mavis what her ceremony was like, and she says that instead of "The Wedding March" she chose K. C. and the Sunshine Band's song "That's the Way— Uh-Huh, Uh-Huh—I Like It" and danced herself down the aisle.

Her husband does a deadpan "Uh-huh, uh-huh."

The music plays. We wait. Mavis whispers that she has to go to the bathroom again. I say, "Think how much better you'd feel if you had a Depends on right now." This is what I'm saying when Max and Sophie walk down the aisle.

———•———

The reception kicks off with a klezmer band doing their bloop-yatty-bloop, and Sophie and Max are hauled up on chairs for the Jewish wedding version of musical chairs. I was raised as an assimilationist, but it's not my confused identity that prevents me from joining in; I've got the spirit, but I can't clap to the beat.

Finally, we go to our tables. I'm at One, sitting between Mavis and Sophie, and I know everyone at the table except the man taking his seat at the opposite end. He's tall and gangly with olive skin, a high forehead, and big eyes—cute, but that doesn't explain what comes over me. I haven't had this feeling in so long I don't even recognize it; at first I think it's fear. My hair follicles seem to individuate themselves and freeze; then it's like my whole body flushes.

He smiles over at me and mouths, *I'm Robert.*

I mouth, *Jane.*

When I come out of my swoon, Mavis is telling the table that my Depends comment made her pee in her pants. She tells me I should work Tiny into my toast, and only now do I remember that I'm supposed to give one.

I try to think of it during dinner, but I'm also trying not to stare at Robert, and I'm shaky and not exactly prepared when it's my turn to go up to the microphone.

"Hi," I say to the crowd. I wait for something to come

to me, and then I see Sophie and it does. I say that we met after college in New York, and that over the years we had a succession of boyfriends but weren't so happy with any of them. We were always asking each other, "Is this all we can expect?"

"Then," I say, "there was our sea-horse period, when we were told that we didn't need mates; we were supposed to make ourselves happy just bobbing around in careers.

"Finally, Sophie met Max," I say, and turn serious. I look over at him. I think, He has a nice face. And I say this into the microphone. "He gets how funny and generous and wholehearted she is. He understands what a big person she is, and yet he doesn't want to crush her." I get some blank stares here, but Sophie's laughing. I say, "Max is the man Sophie didn't know if she could hope for."

When I sit down, Robert stands, I assume to give his toast. But he walks over to my side of the table and asks Mavis if she'll trade seats with him.

She says, "No," and waits a moment before relinquishing her chair.

Robert sits beside me and says, "I loved your toast."

I linger over the word *love* coming out of his mouth about something of mine.

He tells me that he knows Max from freshman year— roughly twenty years—and I remember that a huge number of Oberlin friends are here and ask what bonds them all for life.

He says, "No one else will be friends with us."

Then another toaster picks up the microphone.

Toast, toast, toast; Robert and I can talk only during the intermissions in hurried exchanges: I learn that he's a cartoonist, and I have to tell him that I work in advertising. "But," I say, and don't know what to say next. "I'm thinking of opening a dog museum."

Toast.

"A dog museum?" he says. He's not sure if I'm kidding. "For the different breeds?"

"Maybe," I say. "Or else it could be a museum that dogs would enjoy. It could have interactive displays of squirrels dogs could chase and actually catch. And a gallery of scents."

Toast.

He tells me he's just moved back to New York from L.A. and is staying with his sister until he finds an apartment. I tell him I live in Sophie's old apartment in the huge ancient building nicknamed the Dragonia for its gargoyles. Almost everyone knows someone who has lived there—an ex-girlfriend or masseuse, a cousin—and Robert does, too, though he doesn't specify whom.

Toast.

Will I check on vacancies for him? I will.

Sophie's father goes up to the microphone for the last toast, a position of honor he's requested. He reads a rhyming poem:

> "I despaired at my spinster daughter
> though I thought her
> awfully fair.
> Then came Maxie, praise the Lord,
> from the heavens, I had scored."

Sophie's shaking her head; Max is trying to smile at his father-in-law. Robert leans over and whispers to me,

> "Dad is trying awfully hard,
> but this guy is no one's bard."

Max and Sophie go table to table to talk to their guests, and as soon as Robert and I have the chance to talk without interruption, a statuesque beauty in a drapey gown interrupts.

"Jane," Robert says, "this is Apollinaire."

I'm about to say, "Call me Aphrodite," but I realize in time that he's not kidding.

"Have a seat," he tells her, nodding to the one next to me. But she gracefully drops beside him, as though to fill her urn, forcing Robert to turn his back to me. It occurs to me that I may not be the only butterfly whose wings flutter in the presence of his stamen.

After she glides off, Robert tells me that she composes music for movies and has been nominated for an Oscar. I think of my only award, an honorable mention in the under-twelve contest to draw Mr. Bubble.

"I like her toga," I say, confusing my ancients.

We talk, we talk, and then Robert announces to the table at large that it's time for us to prepare the newly-weds' getaway car.

Outside it's drizzling. Robert retrieves two grocery bags from the bushes and leads us to Max's car.

Mavis shaving-creams smiley faces on the windows.

"Très droll," her husband says, looking on.

I don't spray a word. I hold my shaving cream poised but nothing comes out. I say that I'm blocked.

Robert, tying cans to the bumper, says, "Just pretend you're spraying in your journal."

As we walk away from the parking lot, he says, "I'm pretty sure that's his car."

———•———

Inside, Sophie says she's bummed a cigarette and we go out to the patio. The tables and chairs are wet, but we manage to hike up her dress so it's just her underpants against the seat, and her big skirt swooping up and over the arms of the chair. She reminds me of a swan.

We have so much to say to each other that only quiet will do. We pass the cigarette back and forth, as we have done a thousand times, until her little niece and nephew run outside and shout, "Everyone's looking for you!"

Sophie hands me the cigarette, and as she gets up, she says, "Watch out for Robert." Before I can ask why, the little ones drag her inside.

Inside, someone is calling out, "Unmarried women! Maidens!" Most of Max and Sophie's friends are single, and a big crowd gathers by the staircase; for the first time in my wedding-going life I stand among them. Sophie appears at the top of the steps. Her eyes widen when she sees me. Trusting nothing to chance, she doesn't even turn her back to the crowd; she tosses the bouquet to me, and I catch it.

Then kissing and rice throwing, and the newlyweds are off to Italy for three weeks.

—•—

It's time for me to go, and I want to say good-bye to Robert, but he's talking to Apollinaire. I catch his eye, and wave, and he excuses himself and comes over.

"You're leaving?" he says.

He walks me out the door and down the path to the parking lot. For the moment the rain has stopped, though the sky hasn't cleared and the trees are full of water.

"This is my car," I say. It's an old VW Rabbit with so many scratches and nicks it looks like it's been in a fight.

He stands at the passenger door; I'm at the driver's. He seems to be waiting for something, and I say, "I'd like to invite you in, but it's a mess."

The front seats are covered with old wet towels because the convertible top leaks, and the floor is littered with fast-food wrappers from the last dozen road trips I've taken.

I tell him that the garbage and rags discourage thieves, and if the trash doesn't deter them, there's the wet-poodle smell.

"You have a poodle?" he says.

"A standard," I say. "Jezebel."

He grew up with standard poodles and loves them, and what color is mine? I think that I have found the only straight man in the world who loves poodles.

He tells me he has a cat.

"A cat?" I say. "How can you do that?"

"I love her," he says. "But we both know she's just a placeholder."

Then there's a rush of drops—at first I think it's from the trees, but it's real rain, total rain, and Robert pulls his jacket up over his head and runs over to my side, kisses my cheek, and gallops back to the mansion, presumably into Apollinaire's widespread wings.

I sit on the wet rags and try not to feel like a wet rag myself.

Then he's knocking on my window. I roll it down. He says, "Can I call you," and I answer "Sure" so fast that my voice overlaps the rest of his sentence "about the Dragonia?"

"Sure," I say again, pretending I didn't say it the first time. "I'm in the phone book," I say. "Rosenal."

"Rose 'n' Al, Rose 'n' Al, Rose 'n' Al," he says fast, and disappears.

——•——

He doesn't call on Sunday.

Monday, between writing lines, "Call now for your free gift," and "There's never been a better time to call," I call home to check my answering machine. I feel elated dialing, despondent when I hear the inhuman voice say, "No new messages." Then I call again.

Donna calls to ask about the wedding, and I tell her about Robert. It feels good just to say his name, like he's still a clear and present danger. Then I have to say, "But he hasn't called."

She says, "Why don't you call him?"

I don't answer.

My devoted friend says, "I don't think you could have felt so strongly if he didn't feel the same way about you."

I say, "How do you feel about Jeremy Irons?"

—— • ——

When I get home, the machine's red light is blinking. I say, "Please be Robert." It is. His voice is low and shy, saying he's on his way out and will call back.

I play the message again and watch Jezebel's face. "What do you think?" I ask her.

She looks back at me: *I think it's time for my walk.*

We go around the block and are almost home when we run into a dog we haven't met before, a beautiful weimaraner. Jezebel goes right up to him and licks his mouth. The weimaraner jumps back. "He's a little skittish," his owner says, led away by Herr Handsome.

"I can't believe you just walked up and kissed him," I say to Jezebel, "without even sniffing his butt first."

I make a salad. I try to start another Edith Wharton novel, but I can't concentrate in the silence of the phone not ringing.

Then I think, What if he does call? I'll just mess it up. The only relationships I haven't wrecked right away were the ones that wrecked me later.

I don't admit to myself what I'm doing when I put my bike helmet on and ride over to the Barnes & Noble a few blocks away. I pretend that maybe I'm just getting another Edith Wharton novel.

But I bypass Fiction and find Self-Help. I think, *Self-Help? If I could help myself, I wouldn't be here.*

There are stacks and stacks of *How to Meet and Marry Mr. Right*, the terrible book Donna told me about, terrible because it works. I take my copy up to the counter as furtively as I would a girdle or vibrator.

——·——

There isn't a photograph of the authors, Faith Kurtz-Abromowitz and Bonnie Merrill, but after only a few pages, I see them perfectly. Faith is a reserved blown-dry blonde; Bonnie, a girly-girl, a giggler with deep dimples. I have known them my entire life: in gym class, playing volleyball, they were the ones clapping their hands and shouting, "Side out and rotate—our team is really great!" In college, Bonnie was my Secret Santa. In personnel offices, when I joked about my application phobia, Faith was the one who said, "Just do the best you can."

Now I am turning to them for guidance.

Still, they promise that if you follow their advice, "You will marry the man of your dreams!" and I read on.

Their premise is that men are natural predators, and the more difficult the hunt, the more they prize their prey.

In other words, the last thing you want to do is tap a hunter on the shoulder and ask him to shoot you.

Half of me has to make fun of the book, if only because I've broken all of their rules—"vows," they call them—the other half is relieved that I haven't broken any with Robert yet.

I read the book from bold blurb to bold blurb until I get to **Don't be funny!**

I think, Don't be funny?

"Right," I hear smooth, stoical Faith say. "Funny is the opposite of sexy."

"But I'm attracted to funny men," I say.

Bouncy Bonnie says, "We're not talking about who *you're* attracted to, silly! Go out with clowns and comedians if you want to! Laugh your head off! Just don't make any jokes yourself!"

"Men like femininity," Faith says, crossing her legs. "Humor isn't feminine."

"Think of Roseanne!" Bonnie says.

"Or those fat, knee-slapping girls from *Hee Haw*," Faith adds dryly.

"What about Marilyn Monroe?" I say. "She was a great comic actress."

"That's probably why there's a lingerie line named after her," Faith says.

I say, "But Robert likes me because I am funny."

"You don't know why he likes you," Faith says.

Bonnie says, "You looked terrific in that sheath!"

I hate this book. I don't want to believe it. I try to think what I do know about men. What comes to mind is an account executive at work saying, "Ninety-nine percent of men fantasize about having sex with two women at once."

My mother hardly ever gave me advice about men, and I only remember asking her once, in fifth grade. I'd dispatched a friend to find out if the boy I liked liked me. "Bad news," my friend reported, "he hates you."

My mother kept saying, "What's wrong, Puss?" I couldn't tell her. Finally, I asked how you got a boy you liked to like you back. She said, "Just be yourself," as though I had any idea who that might be. At a loss, my poor mother suggested I jump on my bike and ride around the block to put roses in my cheeks.

—•—

My brother calls inviting me to a benefit for a theater company Friday night—his girlfriend, Liz, knows the director. "It's a singles event," Henry says.

"Singles?" I say. I think of individually wrapped American cheese slices.

"There's some theme," he says.

"Desperation?" I suggest.

He holds the phone and asks Liz what the theme is.

I hear her say, "It's a square dance."

"A square dance?" he says, in a you're-kidding tone.

"Don't say it like that," she says. "Let me talk to her." She gets on the phone. "Jane?" she says.

"Hi."

"It sounds dorky," Liz says, "but I went last year and it was really fun!"

It occurs to me that I might not like fun.

"You want to meet men," Faith says.

Bonnie says, **"Say yes to everything you're invited to!"**

"What else were you going to do Friday night?" Faith says calmly. "I think we're talking about Edith Wharton—am I right?"

I'm getting the address of the party when my call waiting beeps. It's Robert. "Hi," I say, flustered. "I'm on another call."

Faith says, "Say you'll call him back."

But I'm confused—isn't this my fish on the line?

"Not yet," Faith says. "He's just nibbling at bait."

I ask Robert if I can call him back.

He says that he's at a pay phone.

"So what?" Bonnie says. "It's a quarter!"

But I say, "Hold on a sec," to Robert and tell Liz I'll see her at the hoedown.

Robert and I talk about how much fun the wedding was. I'm distracted, trying to follow the vows or at least not to break any, but the only ones that come to mind are: **Don't say "I love you" first! Wear your hair long! Don't bring up marriage!**

He tells me he's in the Village, he's been looking at apartments, and asks if I want to meet for coffee.

Bonnie says, **"Don't accept a date less than four days in advance!"**

I stall, asking him how the apartments were, until the recorded voice of an operator comes on the line, asking for another nickel or our call will be terminated.

He adds a nickel. "Terminated sounds so permanent," he says. "So final."

I think, *Not if you believe in the aftercall.* But Faith says, "No jokes."

"So," he says, "do you want to get some coffee?"

I make myself say, "I can't."

"Good girl," Faith says.

"Oh," he says. Pause. Then he asks if I want to have dinner Friday.

"You have plans," Faith says. "Say it."

"I can't Friday," I say.

He goes right by it and asks about Saturday.

"Fine," Faith says.

"Okay," I say to Robert.

Then the operator comes on again, asking for another nickel.

He says, "Listen to her pretending that she didn't interrupt us before."

I am fizzy with elation.

———•———

After therapy, I'm on the elevator when Bonnie says, "That was great!"

"What?" I say.

"You kept the vow **Don't tell your therapist about the guide!**"

"Because I want her to think I'm improving," I say. "I'm hoping that one day she'll say I'm all better and don't need to come back anymore."

"That same day your dry cleaner will recommend hand washing," Faith says, brushing her hair.

———•———

Thursday night, Robert leaves a message with his sister's phone number; I copy it down and pick up the phone to call him back.

"Not yet," Faith says. "Make him wonder a little."

"Isn't that rude?" I say.

"No," Faith says, "rude is not writing that thank-you note to the gay couple who had you out to Connecticut three weeks ago."

"I don't know why you hang out with them anyway!" Bonnie says, looking up from a big bowl of popcorn. "Gay men hate women."

"Excuse me?" I say.

"It's true," Faith says.

"Why am I listening to you?" I say.

Faith says, "Because you don't want to sleep with Edith Wharton for the rest of your life?"

———•———

I call Robert back from work.

"Eight o'clock okay?" he says.

I agree, barely able to keep the thrill out of my voice.

Bonnie points to her little watch and in a singsongy voice says, "Hang up!"

I say, "Look, I have to go."

After I hang up, Bonnie says, "Short conversations! And you be the one who gets off the phone first!"

Faith nods. "Make him long for you."

—•—

The square dance is way on the East Side, in the Twenties, just a gym with a caller in braids. I spot Liz, adorable in overalls, and Henry, still in his suit.

"Howdy-do," I say.

I stand with my brother and Liz. Here I am at a party on a Friday night and I have a date tomorrow. I think, I am a dater; I am a snorkeler in the social swim.

Faith says, "Feels good, doesn't it?"

It does.

Much clapping and stamping and yee-hawing. I can't clap, of course, but I'm about to let out a yee-haw when Faith shakes her head.

"I was just having a good time," I say.

Faith reminds me that that's not what I'm here for.

"This is a singles dance!" Bonnie says, clapping right in time.

Liz says that we should be dancing, and when I agree, she takes it upon herself to find a partner for me.

The guy she brings back is Gus, the stage manager, a big teddy bear with a fuzzy face and teeth so tiny they make him appear not to have any.

He's aware of performing a kindness; he seems to regard me as poor, plain Catherine from *Washington Square* or poor, sick Laura from *The Glass Menagerie*.

He takes my hand and leads me danceward.

"Bow to your partner," Braidy says. "Ladies, curtsy."

When Gus and I promenade, he smiles encouragement at me, like I'm Clara from *Heidi* and he's teaching me how to walk. But I suddenly remember square dancing in gym circa third grade, and it's the nine-year-old in me swinging my partner and do-si-doing.

"Great!" Bonnie says.

Faith offers up a restrained, "Yee-haw."

After dancing, I'm about to say, *I'm parched as a possum,* but Faith interrupts: "Say, 'Let's get something cold to drink,' " and those are the words I say.

"Sure," Gus says.

We go to the beer-sticky bar, and Faith says, "Ask him what a stage manager does."

"Men love to talk about themselves!" Bonnie says.

So I ask, and he says, "I do what no one else wants to do."

I'm told to smile as though captivated.

Sipping a beer herself, Faith says, "Now let him do the work."

I am only too happy to oblige.

Bonnie says, "Let your eyes wander around the dance floor!" But this seems unkind.

"He's a prospect," Faith says, "not a charity."

I look around, and Gus, trying to regain my attention, asks if I'd like to dance again.

Bonnie says, "One dance per customer."

Instead of saying a jokey *Much obliged, but I should*

join my kin, I anticipate Faith and say, "It was nice meeting you, Gus."

Like a caller herself, Bonnie says, **"Circulate!"** And
I do.

Faith says, "Do not establish eye contact."

"Really?" I say.

"You think that's the only way to get a man to notice
you, don't you?" she says.

"You poor lamb!" Bonnie says.

I've never acknowledged this even to myself. I sound
pathetic.

"Yes," Faith says, "especially because nothing is more
compelling to a man than a lack of interest."

To my astonishment, she's right. Men appear out of
nowhere and glom on to me. Bonnie and Faith tell me
what to do, and I obey: I refuse a second dance with a
man I'm actually attracted to; I don't enter the pie-eating
contest; I ask questions like "What kind of law do you
practice?"

By the end of the night, my phone number is in a
half-dozen pockets. "This never happened to me before,"
I tell Faith.

She says, "I know I should feign surprise."

When my brother and Liz walk me to my bike, he
says, "Who were those guys you were talking to?"

"Who knows?" I say, giddy with the freedom to make
jokes. "I feel like the belle of the ball."

He says, "The ho of the hoedown."

"You know what just occurred to me?" I say, laughing. "I went to a singles square dance in a gym, to meet men."

When Liz says, "You can't think that way," I'm reminded of Faith in personnel saying, "Just do the best you can."

I wonder if my brother is going to marry her.

———•———

Right before Robert arrives, Bonnie says, "Don't be too eager!" When I look in the mirror, my smile is huge and my eyes bugged out with anticipation. I tell myself to think of death. When that doesn't work, I think of yesterday's brainstorming session to name a new auto club for frequent drivers.

Robert buzzes. I open the door and he looks as excited as I did a moment before. He sees Jezebel and gets on his knees and rubs her haunches. "Jezzie," he says.

"Do you want a glass of wine?" I ask.

He does.

He follows me into the kitchen. He says he's still in apartment-hunting mode, and do I mind if he looks around?

"Go ahead," I say, and he goes.

He asks if I've had a chance to check on vacancies in my building, and I'm reminded of Erich von Stroheim in *Sunset Boulevard* saying, "It wasn't Madame he wanted, it was her car."

"I'm sorry—I haven't," I say, and if I were in one of his cartoons, there would be icicles hanging from my balloon.

Maybe he hears it, because he's quiet a moment. He walks around my living room and stops at the table with my little cardboard barnyard animals on their wooden stands. He picks up each one—the bull, the lamb, the pig, and the cow—and reads the breed information on the back. I say that I found them at a flea market in the Berkshires; I pictured little farm kids coming in from their chores to play with their cardboard cows and lambs. I'm about to explain what I find moving and also funny, but I see that I don't have to.

He goes to my bookshelves and notices my portable typewriters from the fifties. He whispers their names, "Silent" and "Quiet Deluxe," which is what I did when I first saw them.

—•—

Over dinner, at a goofy little French place in the neighborhood, he asks how I got into advertising.

Bonnie says, **"Don't be negative!"**

"It started as a day job," I say. I tell him that I thought I'd write plays or novels or appliance manuals at night. But advertising made my IQ go down; every night I had to work just to get it back up to regular.

"What did you do?" he asks.

I got rid of my TV, I tell him, and read classics.

"Like which ones?"

"*Middlemarch* was the first," I say.

He laughs. "You say it like you're not sure I've heard of it."

We keep talking books, and when I tell him that *Anna*

Karenina is my favorite, it seems to have the effect "I'm not wearing any underwear" has on other men.

I say, "The good thing about reading is that you never get blocked—and every page is really well written." He smiles, but seriously, and I can tell that he hears what I'm not saying.

I ask about his work, and he says that it's hard to describe cartoons—you wind up just saying the plot, and his cartoons never have any. "I'll show them to you," he says.

When I ask him why he left L.A., he tells me that it was the loneliest place on earth. "Especially when you're hanging out with people," he says. "Everybody smiles at your jokes."

He loves New York, he says. "It's like Oberlin—it's where people who don't belong anywhere belong."

Only when Faith tells me to stop gazing at Robert do I realize that I am. I look down at his hand on the table. I see the indent where he holds his pen is slightly darkened from ink he couldn't wash off.

Bonnie says, "Ask if he uses a computer."

"You don't use a computer?" I say, which seems like the most mundane question I could ask.

"Just for the animation," he says. "I'm a Luddite, like you, on your—" he whispers, "—Quiet Deluxe."

I don't know what a Luddite is, but Bonnie won't let me ask.

When the check comes, Faith says, "Don't even look at it."

"Let him pay!" Bonnie says.

"What are you thinking about?" Robert asks, putting his credit card in the leatherette folder. "Eighty-seven fifty for your thoughts."

"Be mysterious!" Bonnie says.

"Excuse me," I say, and go to the ladies' room.

"The red wine stained your teeth a little," Bonnie says, handing me a tissue. "Just rub the front ones."

"Listen," I say to them, "I appreciate what you're trying to do for me, but I think I'm better off on my own with Robert."

"Last night wasn't a fluke," Faith says.

"But Robert's different," I say.

"The only difference is that you want him," Faith says.

—•—

On the way home, Robert takes my hand in his, not lacing our fingers, but really taking ownership of my whole hand.

"Let go of his hand first," Faith says.

I love holding hands. In my entire dating life I have never let go first.

"You can do it," Faith says, and I make myself.

Bonnie says, "Let him be the lovesick puppy!"

At my door, instead of asking if he can come in, Robert asks if he can take Jezebel out with me.

"On our first date?" I say.

"If you let me," he says, "I'll respect you even more."

Outside, he meets the neighborhood dogs—and says

what I always do: "Can I say hello to your dog?" His favorites are my favorites—Flora, the huge bulldog; Romeo, the harlequin Great Dane.

I think, *You love dogs as much as I do.*

Back at my apartment, I take Jezebel off her leash, and in my mini-vestibule, he leans toward me and we kiss.

"The date ends now," Faith says. "It's not going to get better."

"Okay," I say in my love daze. "Good night, Robert."

His eyes look disappointed, and I want to touch his hand or pull him toward me, but Bonnie says, **"Keep him guessing!"** And I do.

———•———

He calls the next morning while I'm walking Jez. "Hi, girls," his message says. "I wondered if you wanted to go to the dog run."

There's nothing I want to do more, but I know that I can't.

Bonnie actually gives me a hug.

"I want to see you," Robert says when he calls later.

My whole body hears these words.

He asks when we can get together, and though I think, *Right now is too long to wait,* I say, "Friday?"

"Next Friday?" he says, crestfallen.

"High five," Bonnie says, and slaps hands with Faith.

Robert says, "Do you like me at all?"

"Yes, I like you."

"A lot?" he asks.

Faith tells me to pause before answering, and I do. "Yes."

"Good," he says. "Don't stop."

Bonnie sings, "Who can turn the world on with her smile?"

———•———

Robert calls me at the office and calls me at home. He calls just to say good morning and good night.

One night, he calls to tell me he thinks he's found an apartment only a few blocks from mine and wants me to see it.

I want to so badly it hurts. I tell Robert that I wish I could. I wonder when I can be normal again.

"You're normal now," Faith says.

"You were screwed up before!" Bonnie says.

Faith says, "If you were being your normal self, he wouldn't even be calling you now."

"All right," Robert says. "I guess I'm going to sign the lease." Then: "You don't feel like I'm stalking you, do you?"

———•———

I meet Donna for a drink and admit that I read the book she told me about—the fishing manual.

"Isn't it the worst?" she says.

"I know," I say.

"All those exclamation points," she says. "It can't apply to New York."

"The thing is," I say, "it's working."

"You're actually doing it?" Then she says, "I don't

know why I say it like that—I tried it myself." She tells me that she kept pretending to be aloof, but men didn't seem to notice. "Maybe it was the men I was meeting," she says. "Cabdrivers," and she imitates herself nonchalantly giving an address.

I tell her about my date with Robert and that now he's calling me all the time and he's actually moved into my neighborhood.

"No!" she says, mocking my distress.

"But it's like I'm tricking him into it," I say.

She says, "Well, what about all those guys who act like they're in love with you to get you into bed? Like Fuckface."

"But," I say. I'm having trouble saying what I mean. "I want this to be real."

She says, "Was it more real when he wasn't calling you?"

———•———

I'm getting ready for my date with Robert when Faith says, "Try not to make so many jokes this time."

"Listen," I say, "funny is the best thing I am."

Faith says, "Making jokes is your way of saying *Do you love me?* and when someone laughs you think they've said yes."

This gives me pause.

Faith says, "Let *him* court *you*."

Bonnie hands me my deodorant. "You can be as funny as you want *after* he proposes!"

Robert arrives early, saying he wants to take me to a

play. He has brought a stick for Jezebel to chew, and she gives him the loving look I wish I could.

I pour a glass of wine for him and go back to the bathroom to finish drying my hair. "Now this is a real date!" Bonnie says.

I say, "Your idea of a real date probably ends in a carriage ride through Central Park."

"Her point is that he started by asking to meet for coffee," Faith says. "Now he's trying to win you."

Through the motor of my blow-dryer I hear the phone ring, and when I come into the living room Robert's staring down at the machine, frowning. Gus is asking if I'd like to go out for dinner next week.

Robert looks over at me. "She can't," he says to the machine. "Sorry."

——•——

We go to *Mere Mortals,* a collection of one acts by David Ives. The one I love the most is about two mayflies on a date; they watch a nature documentary about themselves and discover their life span is only one day long—after mating, they'll die.

Leaving the theater, Robert and I are both dazzled and exuberant, talking at once and laughing, and we spontaneously kiss.

He says, "I want to mate with you and die."

We have a drink at one of those old-fashioned restaurants in the theater district. Robert says the mayflies play is what every cartoon he draws aspires to be—beautiful and funny and sad and true.

"I want to see them," I say.

"Okay," he says, and takes out a piece of paper.

It's a pen-and-ink drawing of Jezebel, and I think, *You are the man I didn't know I could hope for.*

"Relax," Faith says. "It's a sketch."

———•———

Back at my apartment, we begin to mate with our clothes on, lying on the sofa on top of shards of chewed-up stick.

At first Faith's voice is no more than a distant car alarm. But it gets louder and I hear her say, "No."

"Yes," I say to her.

"You don't want to lose him," she says, in the voice you'd use to talk someone on acid out of jumping out a window. "The way you've lost every man you've really wanted."

I sigh inwardly and pull back.

"What?" he says.

I tell him that I'm not ready to sleep with him yet.

"Okay," he says, and pulls me back to him. We go on kissing and touching and moving against each other for another few minutes, and then he says, "Are you ready now?"

Here is a man who can make my body sing and make me laugh at the same time. "Which is why you don't want to lose him," Faith says.

———•———

Over the phone, he tells me that his ex-girlfriend called him today. I picture Apollinaire.

I want to ask who she is and how he feels about her,

but Faith practically takes the phone from me. Instead, I ask how long ago he went out with her.

Almost a year ago and she's why he left New York. "She sort of decimated me." He asks if I'd mind signing a nondecimation pact.

I'm choosing which of my own decimation experiences to relate, but Bonnie says, "He doesn't need to know about that!"

———•———

We meet for a drink at the café between our apartments. He asks what I wish I could do instead of advertising.

I think, *I'd like to make pasta necklaces and press leaves; I didn't really appreciate kindergarten at the time.* But I just shake my head.

He says, "Let's make a list of what you think would be fun to do."

"No," Faith says. "Don't let him think you need help."

"I do need help," I say.

"He'll think you're a loser!" Bonnie says. With her thumb and index finger she makes an L, pinches and opens it fast: the flashing Loser sign.

———•———

He doesn't call the next morning, afternoon, or night, and, needless to say, I can't call him.

Friday night, we go to the movies as planned, but he doesn't hold my hand in the dark theater, doesn't kiss me on the cab ride home. I want to ask him what's wrong, but Faith says not to. "It shows how much you care."

When the cab pulls up to the Dragonia, he tells me he's tired. He doesn't ask if I have plans for Saturday night.

Saturday night, I read until midnight. When I take Jezebel out for her last walk, I go all the way to his street, and down the dark side. He and Apollinaire are sitting on his stoop.

I am shaking when I get home.

—•—

Sunday, when the phone rings I run for it. But it's a crush from college, Bill McGuire—nicknamed "Mac." He lives in Japan and says he'll be coming to New York next weekend and wants to take me out for dinner Saturday.

I hesitate.

Bonnie says, **"Get out there!"**

"I've been out there," I say. "Now I want to stay in with Robert."

"He's not staying in!" Bonnie says.

"I don't know that," I say.

"You saw them!" Bonnie says.

"They could just be friends," I say.

"Friends?" Bonnie says.

"He went to Oberlin!" I say.

"Regardless," Faith interrupts, "hunters like competition. It tells them that what they want is worth having."

"But I would feel terrible if he went on a date with someone else," I say.

"And you're trying to date by example?" Faith says.

"It doesn't work like that!" Bonnie says.

I agree to dinner, but as soon as I hang up, I say, "This feels wrong."

"It's right," Faith says, unzipping her dress. "It's just unfamiliar."

"No," I say. "It feels wrong."

She's wearing a slinky, champagne silk slip with spaghetti straps. "Aren't you being pursued the way you always wanted to be?" Faith says.

"I was," I say.

"This'll help," Faith says decisively.

"I hope you're right," I say. "That's a pretty slip."

"You should get one!" Bonnie says.

———•———

The day after Sophie gets back from Italy, we meet for coffee at a café in the Village. Before she tells me about her honeymoon, she asks what's going on with Robert.

I tell her that I don't know. "I think maybe he's seeing someone else."

She says, "What?"

"I saw him with the statue from your wedding," I say. "Apollinaire—the goddess of NASA."

"Apple's a lesbian, okay?" she says. "Besides, he's in love with you. The question is, are you in love with him?"

I nod.

"So, why are you making him so crazy?" she says. "He's not even sure you like him."

I hesitate before breaking the vow **Don't talk to non-guide girls about the guide!** Then I tell her everything.

For a second she looks at me like I'm someone she used to know. "Are you serious?"

"I know how it sounds," I say. I try to think how to explain. I borrow Donna's swimming-versus-fishing analogy. "I realized I didn't know anything about men."

She says, "You didn't know about manipulation."

I say, "Tell me I haven't wrecked every relationship I've ever been in."

She says something about the unworthiness of my ex-boyfriends.

"I don't want to wreck it with Robert," I say, and I admit that I don't think the book is all wrong.

"What's it right about?" she says.

"Well," I say. "Max made the first move, right?"

She says, "Max is a slut."

"And he pursued you," I say. "You didn't even return his calls."

"I thought he was insane," she says.

I persist. "And he said 'I love you' first."

"On our first date," she says. "He's like you—or how you used to be—"

I say, "Well, those are all vows from the book."

"Vows?" She shakes her head. "You need de-programming."

She bums a cigarette from our waitress, and I remember to ask why she warned me about Robert.

She hesitates. "I thought of him as a commitment-phobe. But now I'm more worried about you. You have to stop reading that book."

"I haven't read it in weeks," I say. "I internalized it—
you know how susceptible I am." I remind her of the
time I borrowed an ancient typing manual from the library; I kept typing a practice exercise about the importance of good grooming in job interviews. I say, "Every
time I go on one I still think 'Neatly combed hair and
clean fingernails give a potential employer—' "

She interrupts me. "You need an antidote." She suggests Simone de Beauvoir.

———•———

I'm reading *The Second Sex* when Faith says, "My husband was a total commitment-phobe."

"Really?" Bonnie says.

Faith says, "Lloyd didn't have a girlfriend the whole
four years he was in medical school."

I say, "Maybe he was studying all the time."

"Yeah," she says, "studying pussy."

Bonnie's nose wrinkles. "Faith!"

"The point is," Faith says, "the guide is about getting
commitment-phobes to commit."

"I'm trying to read," I say.

"Did you ever read her letters to Sartre?" Faith says.
"Pathetic."

I ignore her.

She says, "You'll notice that she never became Madame
Sartre."

"Look," I say, "I'm not thinking about marriage anymore. I just want to be with Robert."

Faith says, "You sound just like Simone."

—— • ——

Friday, Robert takes me to dinner at the Time Café, a hipster restaurant, and we're seated across from a table of models.

He doesn't even seem to notice them, and against Faith's protests, I tell him with my eyes how I feel.

I can see he's surprised—he practically says, *Me?*

I say, "You."

"Me, what?" he says.

I say, "Will you make love to me after dinner?"

Bonnie says, "I can't believe you."

Faith gets the waitress and orders a double martini.

Robert moves the table aside and comes over to me on the sofa, and we kiss and don't stop until our salads come.

He eats his with theatrical speed. "Let's take Jezebel and go to the country tomorrow."

"Yes," I say.

Robert tells me that Apple invited us to her girlfriend's place in Lambertville, and all he has to do is call them.

Bonnie says, "You have a date tomorrow, kiddo."

I taste the vinegar in my salad.

Once our plates are cleared, I excuse myself and go to the phone. I dial Information. I feel bad canceling on Mac, but when the operator asks, "What listing, please?" I feel even worse. I don't know where he's staying.

During dinner I try to convince myself that I could just not show up for my date. But I know I'm not capable of this.

"Robert," I say finally, "I can't go away with you."

"Why?" he says.

I can't make my mouth form the words. I start to. I say, "I have a . . ." and Robert says, "You have a date."

He shakes his head for a minute. Then he signals for the waitress. While he signs the credit-card slip, I blather on about how the guy is from Japan, and I would cancel but— He interrupts me with a look.

"Two stops," he says to the cabdriver.

Faith says, "Nice going."

—— • ——

In the morning, I call Robert; his phone rings and rings. I take Jezebel to the dog run at Madison Square Park. It is the first true day of summer, but the clear sky and strong sun just make New York seem gritty.

Even the sight of Jezebel prancing around doesn't cheer me up. I feel like the old whiny beagle none of the dogs will play with.

"I know how hard this is," Faith says. "But if Robert is so easily discouraged, he's not right for you anyway."

I say, "If Robert did this to me, I'd try to forget about him."

"You're putting yourself in his place," Faith says.

"You're not Robert!" Bonnie says. "You're not a man!"

"I'm a dog," I say, "and you're trying to make me into a cat."

—— • ——

I wash my hair. Dry it. I put on a dress and sandals. Drop lipstick in my bag. I do it all as perfunctorily as if I were preparing for an appointment with my accountant.

Bonnie says, "Look at your nails! You could repot a geranium with what's under there!"

"What is it with you people and nails?" I say irritably.

I put on my bicycle helmet.

"You're not riding your bicycle," Bonnie says. "He'll think you're a weirdo."

"I am a weirdo, Bonnie."

"Well," she says, "you don't have to wear it on your sleeve or whatever."

I see Mac before he sees me. He's tall with broad shoulders and wavy blond hair, aristocratic in a blue blazer and white shirt. His strange features—beady eyes, thin lips, and a pointy chin—somehow conspire to make him attractive, though I feel none of the electricity of yesteryear.

"Jane Rosenal," he says, and as he kisses my cheek I realize that for all of our flirting we never kissed.

He looks down at my helmet. "Bicycle?"

"Yup," I say.

"Isn't it dangerous?" he says.

I nod.

"Do you mind eating outside?" he asks.

We follow the maître d' upstairs to an exquisite roof garden with candles and flowers, flowers everywhere. It's breezy and the sky is full of billowy clouds, and for a moment I am not sorry to be here. Then I remember Robert and the cost of this dinner.

"Do you want a bottle of wine?" Mac asks.

"I think I'll have a drink-drink," I say, and when the waiter comes I order a martini. Mac says he'll have the same.

"So," he says and begins to ask the questions you'd expect. He speaks and then I do, his turn, then mine; it's less like a conversation than a transatlantic call.

He says that he lives in a residence hotel for businessmen, which is convenient and luxurious; and it isn't until he adds, "Home, sweet residence hotel, I guess," that I realize he's funny, dry and deadpan, his own straight man.

"By the way," he says, "you can call me Mac if you want to, but I go by William now."

"I go by Princess Jane," I say. "If we get to know each other better, I may let you call me just Princess."

He laughs. "That's what I remember about you," he says. "You were so funny."

"See?" I say to Bonnie and Faith.

"And it only took him fifteen years to call," Faith says.

———•———

After two martinis and a bottle of wine with dinner, I realize I better order coffee if I want to walk down the steps.

During dessert, Mac asks if he can call me Princess, and I say, "Yes, William."

He tells me that he plans to come back from Asia before long; he wants to teach in Morristown, New Jersey, the horsy suburb where he grew up.

"What would you teach?" I ask.

"Anything but gym," he says. "What about you, Princess? Can you see yourself growing old in the suburbs?"

I know what he's asking, and the Faith and Bonnie in me is glad to hear it. But I say, "Only if it's a choice between the suburbs and setting myself on fire."

Outside, he suggests we go somewhere to get a drink or hear music. "No, thank you," I say. I tell him that I have to walk my bicycle, and if I start now I'll just make it home before sunrise.

"Can I kiss you?" he asks.

I shake my head. I'm about to say that my lips are spoken for, but with a pang I realize that they are not. I say, "You can unlock me," and I hand him the key.

He unlocks my bicycle and says, "We'll put it in a cab."

He hails one, and maneuvers my bicycle into the trunk. I get in the cab and thank him for dinner. He nods and says, "My pleasure."

I say, "You have a nice personality." Then I give the driver my address.

———•———

No messages on the machine. I take Jezebel out and walk her to Robert's building. I look up at the windows and try to guess which are his.

"Go home, pumpkin," Bonnie says.

I sit on the stoop. Jezebel maneuvers herself so she can lie beside me, and puts her head on my lap.

To the tune of "Why Can't a Woman Be More Like a Man?" I whisper, "Why can't a man be more like a poodle?"

"You've had too much to drink," Faith says. "If you want to, you can call him in the morning."

I say, "You're just saying that so I'll go home."

———•———

In the morning, there's still no answer at Robert's.

In the afternoon, when the phone rings I run for it. "Princess?" Mac says. He tells me he had a great time.

"Same here," I say.

After we hang up, Bonnie pats my knee. "Isn't it nice just to hear the phone ring?"

———•———

I picture Robert in the country with Apollinaire and her girlfriend. "Robert, please," she's saying, "the woman's in advertising, for Christ's sake."

Maybe they've invited a date for Robert, a straight, statuesque Oscar nominee.

"You're losing it!" Bonnie says. "You're the one who had the date!"

In the evening, I call Robert again, and this time he picks up the phone. I say, "Aren't you supposed to be stalking me?"

"I went away," he says, and his voice is flat.

I ask if he'll meet me at the outdoor café between our apartments, and he agrees.

After we hang up, I go to the mirror, and Bonnie hands me my lipstick. Faith sits on the ledge of the tub, and reaches for an emery board. She files her nails, stops, and looks up at me. "This is the deciding moment in the hunt," she says.

"This is New York," I say. "Nobody hunts!"

"You don't have to get snappy," Bonnie says. "It's just an analogy."

"No more hunting or fishing," I say.

Faith says, "Just being yourself, is that it?"

"No!" Bonnie says, frowning so hard her dimples show.

"Yes," I say.

"You're going to lose him, Jane," Faith says.

"I won't."

"Yes," Faith says. "You will."

"Okay, but I'll lose him my way," I say.

"That's the spirit," Faith says.

I close my eyes. "I want you to go now."

Faith says, "We're already gone," and when I open my eyes they are. The bathroom is suddenly empty and quiet. I am on my own.

———•———

At the café, Robert is sitting outside, looking at the menu.

He half rises and kisses my cheek, as though we've already broken up and are starting a friendship, which throws me.

"How are you?" I say.

"Fine," he says. "You?"

I nod.

We both order red wine. I say, "Where'd you go?"

He doesn't answer right away. "I went to New Jersey. To my parents' house," he says, sounding like he wishes he could say anyplace else.

"How was it?" I say.

"The usual," he says. "I watered the lawn, argued with my father, regressed, and aged."

I smile, which he doesn't seem to see.

Our wine comes, and he takes a sip and then another.

"Your mouth's purple," I say.

"Listen," he says. "This isn't going to work out."

"No?" I say.

He looks at Jezebel, who lifts her head to be scratched, and he reaches down.

"Don't pet my dog," I say. "If we're breaking up, you can't touch either of us."

"We can't break up," he says. "You're going out with other people."

"Other person," I say. "From Japan," I add, as though it proves something.

"Whatever," he says.

I say, "I don't want to go out with anyone else." I feel relieved saying these words, until I see that they have no effect on him.

"It's not that," he says.

"What is it?"

He takes a deep breath. "I fell in love with someone else."

"Oh," I say. "Well." I once heard someone describe jealousy as ice water coursing through your veins, but in mine it's more like vomit.

"It's not that you're not great—you are great," he says. "I just thought you were different."

"What do you mean?" I say.

He says, "At the wedding, you seemed different from . . ." He hesitates. ". . . from who you turned out to be."

It takes me a second to realize—he means he fell in love with me! Then I realize he also means he fell out of love with me.

My voice is so low that even I can't hear it; I have to repeat myself. "Who did I turn out to be?"

He shakes his head; I see that he doesn't want to hurt me, which hurts even more. "No," I say, "really, I want to know who I turned out to be."

"Like someone from high school," he says.

I think of Faith and Bonnie in gym.

"Or I felt like I was in high school and I was going after you," he says. "Like I had to earn you or win you or something."

"Yeah," I say.

"We were dating," he says. "I don't even know how to date."

"But I don't either," I say.

He doesn't react. He can't hear me anymore; he's decided who I am, and that I am not for him.

"I know I'm weird," he says, "but for me our relationship started when I met you at the wedding."

"Same," I say.

"You're not the same, though, Jane," he says, and his voice is careful again. "You let me know that I had to ask you out, with notice, for dates. Datey dates."

"Datey dates," I say, though he has no way of knowing this is an expression I use myself.

"It's not that you did anything wrong," he says. "I mean, you're the normal one."

"I am not normal," I say to myself.

"I'm sorry," he says, and he means it.

"Who did you think I was?" I say. "At the wedding."

He shakes his head.

"Tell me," I say.

He looks at me as though I'm a good friend, and he lets himself reminisce about the person he was in love with. "You were really funny and smart and open," he says. "You were out there."

"I was out there," I say.

His voice is sad. "Yup."

"Listen," I say. He's sympathetic but I can tell he's wondering how long this will take, and I have to fight myself not to say good-bye and stand. "I got scared," I say.

He seems to hear me, but I don't know which me—maybe just the friend he hopes I'll turn out to be.

"I'm bad at men," I say.

He laughs for the first time in a long while.

"You get all these voices about what a woman is supposed to be like—you know, feminine." I do not want to continue. "And I've spent my whole life trying not to hear them. But . . ." I steel myself to go on. "I wanted to be with you so much that I listened."

He nods, slowly, and I can tell he's starting to see me—the me he thought I was and am.

Still, it takes all of my courage to say, "Show me your cartoons."

On the way to his apartment, I tell him that he can hold Jezebel's leash if he wants to, and he does.

I follow him up the steps to his building, climbing over the ghost of me from last night, up to his apartment on the top floor. Jezebel and I wait outside while he closes the cat in his bedroom. Then he leads us to his study, which has big dormer windows, all of them open, facing the backyard. He asks if I want a glass of wine, and I say yes.

One wall is covered with taped-up cartoons in black ink and watercolor. I find the gallery of scents from my dog museum. Sea horses bobbing. I see cartoon him, up there pining for cartoon me.

He hands me my wine. And I tell him that his cartoons are beautiful and funny and sad and true.

He smiles.

I ask him what else the review of his dreams says about

him. He likes this question. He thinks. Then he says, "Robert Wexler is a goofball in search of truth."

I think, *I'm a truthball in search of goof,* and I realize that I can say whatever I want now. And I do.

Instead of laughing, he pulls me in. We kiss, we kiss, we kiss, in front of Jezebel and all the cartoons. There is no stopping now. Both of us are hunters and prey, fishers and fish. We are the surf 'n' turf special with fries and slaw. We are just two mayflies mating on a summer night.